Healer

Steve Petersen

PUBLISH AMERICA

PublishAmerica
Baltimore

ISBN: 1-4137-2690-9
PUBLISHED BY
PUBLISHAMERICA, LLLP.
www.publishamerica.com
Baltimore

Printed in the United States of America

The following people have contributed to the success of *Healer* more than they will ever know and I wish to thank them from the center of my heart.

Morgan Petersen, my father, has given me his undying support and belief that someday, anything is possible.

My children, Carrie Petersen, Holly Petersen, Jesse Petersen, and April (Petersen) Burns, for their support and acceptance of who I am. Special thanks to April for her hard work on the final editing of *Healer*.

A special thanks to Karl and Kathy Irwin for their dedication to my success.

To all of my family and friends, near and far of heart and field for being always there.

And to all those I will meet because they have chosen to read *Healer*.

Chapter 1
The Stranger

JANUARY 12, 2000: SUSAN Larkin is rushing around the 4,500 square foot Studio City house she and Bill call home. Adrian, their 8-year-old daughter, is playing in her first post-season championship soccer tournament in Mission Viejo. Game time is 6:00 p.m. and the two youngest teams in the tournament are going to start the festivities on the main field of the United States Olympic Soccer Team training facility. Waiting for Adrian's two older brothers to arrive home from school while packing for a weekend down south, made Susan late and anxious to get on the freeway. Fridays are typically bad on Southern California freeways, especially going south on the Golden State toward San Diego.

Bill Larkin is the executive producer of KBLA news at the Los Angeles-based television network. His innovative style and choice of personalities as news reporters has made him one of the top news leaders in local television. Once the weekend programming is completed and the lead stories, as they currently stood, became ready to air, he plans on heading for the field to join his family for a weekend of soccer. Teams, as young as Adrian's, rarely get the opportunity to play on main venue fields, let alone under the lights and Bill has promised not to miss it.

Finally, at 2:40 p.m., Billy, 14, and Eric, 12, arrive home from school hungry.

"Hey, Mom. What's to eat?"

"Yeah, Mom, we're starved," both of the boys chimed in.

"We'll eat in the van, guys. Grab your Quicksilver bags and beach towels then please get in the car, we're late. Use the bathroom before we go." Susan flashed by with her arms loaded as the boys looked on with great disappointment.

"Do we have to go?" they said together. "Can't we stay here with Grandma and Grandpa?"

"No. Your grandparents are going to meet us at the field. Now come on, get your rear ends in the van. We'll drive through McDonald's before we get on the freeway."

Susan made a final check around the house and locked the door. Adrian was already in the front seat and the boys were complaining about her riding shot gun whenever they go to one of her soccer games. Susan ignored them. She double-checked the back of the van just to make sure all of the bags were loaded.

"Adrian, where is your soccer bag?"

"I don't know, Mommy. I couldn't find it."

Susan frowned. "It was in your room when I asked you to look for your soccer ball and put them both in the car."

"I forgot," frowned Adrian.

Susan put her right hand to her forehead. "Eric, jump out and go find your sister's soccer ball. I'll go in the house and get her bag. Come on, son, quickly. Please."

Susan's patience was wearing thin. Of all days to start her period. "Whoever thought of having a soccer game on a Friday afternoon a million miles south of this godforsaken city should have his head examined," grumbled Susan.

Mother and son arrived back at the van at the same time, bag and ball in hand.

"Thank you, son. I will order a Biggy fries just for you."

"Mom, Biggy fries isn't McDonald's, it's Wendy's," Billy said sarcastically.

"Thank you, William." She slammed the double doors forcing everything in the back to squish up against the rear seat.

McDonald's had a line at the drive-through. Susan checked her watch and figured she had no more than ten minutes to wait. It was now 3:15 p.m. If the traffic was still flowing, she would make it to the field with maybe 20 minutes left for Adrian to warm up.

"Welcome to MacDonall. May I have order prease?"

"Pardon me," Susan asked.

"Order prease, what you want prease?" Susan looked back at the boys sternly as they laughed and imitated the person requesting the order.

"We'll have four number one meals, all with Cokes and one with Biggy fries."

"No Biggy Flies. Only Super Size Flies. You want Super Flies?"

"Yes, please." Susan had to say please extra loud to speak over the boys' hysterical laughter.

"You pull for-war now. Pay flast window prease. Thank you come to MacDonall."

Susan pulled forward. A round faced, teenage Asian boy smiled broadly, "Tweney-free fibty-two, prease!"

Susan turned to face the boy in the window after shushing her own boys as they continued to imitate the McDonald's server. For a moment the thought went through her head that the charge of twenty-three dollars and fifty-two cents was rather high. Glancing at her watch, she decided not to make it an issue.

"Here you are, sir," handing him the exact change. "Thank you for your service."

"You welcome, ma'am. Thank you stop at MacDonnall. Prease come gan."

Susan drove to the second window and the food was waiting. She handed the bags over her shoulder to the boys and set the drinks, in their cardboard holder, next to her purse between the seats. She proceeded to the driveway exit and moved quickly into traffic toward the freeway.

"Hey, Mom, they're all super size fries. I thought you said I was the only one that got the super size box," Eric yelled.

"Eric, the boy misunderstood that's all. I'll make it up to you at the soccer field. Billy, would you please pass your sister her food?"

"One order of Biggy Flies coming up."

Adrian turned around in her seat as she scolded Billy. "Stop it, Billy, they aren't flies. They're French fries."

"Adrian, please turn around in your seat and put your seat belt back on. Billy, hand me the food and I'll pass it to your sister. Eric, here's your drink and a straw." Susan was momentarily distracted as she looked for the drink and straw on the floor between the front seats. She had just entered the on ramp to the 101 Freeway East. The speed of the van caused her to move into the turn too fast. She overcorrected the steering and hit the brake. The drink she was just taking out of the paper holder tipped toward her and she pinched the paper cup so tight the lid popped off and Coke ran over the rim, across the driver's side mat, into the step well next to the door.

"Damn it!" She spoke out of frustration more than anger, looking up in time to hit the gas pedal, regaining control and keeping the van from hitting the curb.

"Hey, that's my drink!" Eric cried out.

"You can have my drink, Eric. Stop yelling. Billy, give your brother a napkin please."

Susan handed her Coke back to Eric and he reached up to get his own straw.

Susan had joined the California Highway Patrol after she graduated from college. Her training as a patrol officer made her an excellent driver. She met Bill Larkin at the scene of a traffic accident fifteen years ago and got pregnant during the first six months of their courtship. Bill was making enough money to support the three of them and insisted Susan quit her job. It was their first real test as a couple, after the news of the pregnancy of course. For the next fourteen years Bill's promotions and stock options had made them financially secure. Susan was able to stay home with their children participating in their development, including preschool, grade school, sports, Cub Scouts and Girl Scouts. At times she missed the excitement of the highway patrol but never regretted her decision to be a mother. Fine Arts was Susan's minor in college and with all three children in school it allowed her time to participate, part time, in the procurement of art for the new Thomas B. Rich Museum in Westwood.

Bill and Susan supported several charities in Los Angeles and Susan was active raising money for the Red Cross after the earthquake in 1994. She met Thomas Rich at one of the shelters for the unfortunate newly homeless victims of the quake. He and his right-hand man, Larry Dawkins, were on a tour of the area checking petroleum pipelines, when their car went into a sinkhole on Devonshire Boulevard caused by a broken water main. Members of a rescue crew helped the men to safety and directed them to a nearby Red Cross shelter. The same shelter where Susan Larkin was serving a coordinator for volunteer efforts. Thomas was instantly taken by Susan's straightforward leadership and their conversation led to the project at the new "Thomas B. Rich Museum."

The traffic on the 101 was moving at a steady sixty plus miles per hour. The number of cars on the road was moderate as she drove through Burbank heading toward the 101 and Golden State Freeway interchange. Just before the transition lane started for the 5 freeway south, Eric threw a French fry over the seat into Adrian's hair.

"Who did that? Billy, don't!" Adrian looked over her shoulder.

"I didn't do it, stupid."

"You did too. I'm not stupid, you are." Eric threw another fry.

9

"Billy, stop it!" This time Adrian screamed as loud as she could. Her scream brought Susan out of her daydream.

"Billy!" She looked at him in the rearview mirror. "Leave your sister alone."

"It wasn't me. I swear. It was Er-head." Eric threw another fry and this time it landed in Adrian's lap. It had ketchup dripping on one end and the wet red sauce stood out when it hit Adrian's neon green soccer shorts.

Adrian began to shriek. "Mommy, look at my uniform." Her shriek turned from a sob into hysterical crying.

The traffic on the 5 freeway was heavier but still moving at sixty to sixty-five miles per hour. Susan was in the middle of merging and kept her concentration on the road.

"Mommy, look at me," Adrian screamed.

"I can't right now, Adrian. Just calm down, I can fix it. Eric, don't move a muscle." Adrian turned around in her seat and glared at Eric.

"Adrian, sit down and face the front and put on your seat belt."

Susan passed the exit sign for Stadium Way. She maneuvered around a slow moving sedan with a broken rear window and accelerated into the fast lane. She glanced in the rearview mirror to see if Eric was sitting still and saw his tongue sticking out toward the seat in front of him. Adrian hung over the back of the seat with her tongue wagging back and forth at Eric.

"Adrian, glue your butt into that seat and put your seat belt on, NOW!" She glanced back to the road in front of her and saw what seemed to be a scene from a movie, moving in slow motion.

A semi truck and long bed trailer loaded with steel angle iron was in a sideways skid. The tail of the trailer was sweeping like the second hand of a clock into the fast lane, taking out cars ahead of it as if they were matchbox toys. As the rear trailer tires hit the concrete center divider, they twisted up underneath the bed loaded with steel bars and started to barrel roll. The chain jacks came loose on the first hit and flipped the half-ton bars of steel in the air like pick-up sticks. Sparks flew everywhere. Susan applied the brakes, easily at first, to avoid being hit from a utility truck behind her, in case the driver of the vehicle could not see what was happening directly in front of the Larkin van.

Two bars of angle iron, bound awkwardly by the chains, hit the pavement hard, ricocheting up from the serrated concrete surface and lodged between the chassis and motor of Susan's van. The free ends of the steel sent sparks up from the concrete paving until they hit the under side of the semi trailer now resting on its side across the three outside lanes of freeway. The van stopped as if it hit a wall. Because of the freak nature of the impact, the air bags failed to open. The two boys in the middle seat were held tight to their seats as was Susan, in the driver's seat by their seat belts. Adrian, with her back still facing the front window, was thrown through the windshield head and shoulders first. Her tiny head hitting the concrete, her body flipping as if she were a rag doll, landing limp against the under side of the trailer in front of her. The two boys and their mother were in shock, staring straight ahead watching the scene unfolding before them as if it were a movie.

Traffic stopped in both directions. Several motorists parked their cars and started running toward the van. Two men knelt down by Adrian's body as a man and a woman stood next to the van trying to open the doors on either side. Susan started moving her hands and arms across her face and over to the seat next to her. The windshield was shattered and her daughter was not there.

"Adrian, Adrian, where are you? Adrian, answer me." She was frantic. She looked back at the boys and they were both in their seats looking at her. Eric started to cry. Someone was pounding on the driver's side window asking Susan to unlock the doors, she did and the door swung open. A stranger's face asked her if she was all right. She nodded. A female stranger opened the other side door and asked the boys if they were OK. Eric continued to cry and Billy stared at his mother.

"Can you see my daughter? Is my little girl there by the door?" Susan was pleading for an answer.

The man next to her took her arm and said calmly, "Your little girl was thrown through the windshield. She is out here next to the truck. We called 911 on our cell phone and help is on the way."

"Get out of my way, I want my daughter." Susan pushed past him and saw people kneeling around Adrian's little form lying in the middle of a pile of wreckage. "Get away from her. I'm trained to give emergency medical assistance and she is my daughter."

She pushed and shoved the people trying to help, out of her way. Susan was reacting on pure instinct as she bent over the body of her little girl trying to feel a pulse and putting her ear next to Adrian's mouth to feel or hear a breath. Nothing. She did not try to move her and started giving her mouth to mouth, preparing to begin CPR. There was very little blood coming from the spot where she had hit her head on the ground. Adrian's long blonde hair had been coiled in a braid on her head and must have cushioned the point of impact. Paramedics arrived on the scene the same time as the highway patrol and Los Angeles City Fire Department.

An officer took Susan's arm and tried to move her away so the emergency medical technicians could start working on Adrian. She pulled away. "I'm a trained CHP officer and this is my daughter. I know what I am doing. Stand back, just stand back."

"Susan, Susan Larkin," said a familiar voice. "It's me Ken Taylor. We were in the academy together. Susan, look at me. Please, Susan." Officer Taylor could tell that Adrian's situation was grim.

"Kenny?" Susan looked up helplessly. "Kenny, it's Adrian.

It's my little girl down here. Help me. She's not breathing."

"Susan, let the paramedics do their job. I know these guys, they're the best. Come with me and tell me what happened." Susan was numb and did as he asked.

The fire department paramedics were the best. They had responded to hundreds of freeway accidents on the I-5 and knew when a case was hopeless. Adrian's body was limp and turning blue. Most of the bones in her upper torso were broken. The impact on her head, although almost undetectable, had been fatal. They applied oxygen to her mouth and nose and started an intravenous drip. Speaking softly into the mobile phone patched into the hospital emergency room, they gave the details as they saw them. Trying everything their years of experience had taught them, to no avail.

Susan looked over Ken Taylor's shoulder and saw the look of despair on the paramedics' faces. At first she didn't react and continued to tell about the accident as she remembered it. When one of the medical technicians stood up and shook his head, she broke from Ken's grasp.

"Don't you give up on her. Not now, mister. You stay with her until the ambulance gets here and we will take her to an emergency room." Officer Taylor caught her just as she reached Adrian's body. The paramedic shook his head as the tears started to roll down his cheeks. Susan fell to her knees and pulled Adrian to her chest. First, she stared into her baby girl's ashen face, tears welling in her eyes. She closed her eyes and then she prayed. As she prayed she started rocking back and forth. She ended her silent prayer. She hadn't prayed since she was a little girl in Sunday school. Susan started singing. The air was still. There was no sound except Susan singing "Amazing Grace." Ken Taylor stood to the side with a fireman and watched with wet cheeks of his own. One of the paramedics bent down over Susan Larkin.

"Mrs. Larkin, there are two ambulances here now. One for your two sons as a precaution, and one for you and your daughter."

A stranger pushed by the onlookers and stood quietly looking down at Susan and her daughter. He was dressed in a white T-shirt, faded blue jeans and work boots. He looked about 50 years old and as if he was a construction worker. He watched and listened for a moment. One of the paramedics spoke up.

"Mrs. Larkin? Mrs. Larkin, please let us help you and your daughter to the ambulance." She continued to rock and sing quietly.

The stranger knelt down beside her. He spoke softly, reverently. "Mrs. Larkin, is this your daughter?" Susan looked directly into the stranger's eyes. "Mrs. Larkin, may I hold your daughter?"

Officer Taylor reached for the man and pulled on his left arm. "This is no time for some sick bastard to intrude in a family tragedy." Ken Taylor stood behind the stranger pulling both of his arms until he got the stranger to his feet.

Susan looked deeply at the stranger as if she recognized him. "Kenny, let him go, please." He did. The stranger knelt down again, this time close enough to Susan to touch her side. He took her forearm in his hand guiding her to place Adrian across his legs. He turned to Susan.

"Do you believe, Mrs. Larkin?" The stranger looked directly into her eyes.

"Yes," she said calmly. With that, the stranger put his hands on Adrian's face, closed his eyes and bowed his head. He barely moved his lips, as though uttering a silent prayer. Susan strained to hear his words but could not. The air was still. There was no sound. The stranger placed his hands under Adrian's small head and opened his eyes. Susan continued staring at the man holding her lifeless daughter. With both of her hands she gripped the stranger's left arm and started to cry.

"I believe," in a whisper she repeated, "I do believe." Suddenly, Adrian gasped for air. Her body trembled and started to shake. Adrian reached for her throat and drew in a deep breath. She coughed, breathed again and slowly opened her eyes. She looked directly into the stranger's eyes and relaxed, breathing deeply. Adrian closed and opened her eyes, this time looking at her mother. She stretched out her arms and Susan pulled her to her chest.

"Adrian, Adrian, my baby, you're alive. Oh thank God, my baby is alive." Tears of joy from both mother and daughter mixed as they ran down each other's cheeks. Adrian hugged her mother tightly around the neck. The onlookers stood motionless, unable to grasp what they had seen. Susan opened her eyes and looked toward the stranger. He was gone.

Chapter 2
The Miracle

BILL LARKIN BURST INTO the emergency room. "Where is my family? I'm Bill Larkin. My wife and children were brought in from an automobile accident. Please, can somebody tell me where they are?"

"Yes, Mr. Larkin, I'm the attending nurse, Mrs. O'Neal. Please follow me. Everyone is doing fine. We are just keeping them for observation. You know, just a precaution considering all that happened."

"Exactly what did happen?" Bill asked.

They continued down the hall into a room with four beds. Susan Larkin was standing next to Adrian's bed stroking her hair and holding her left hand. The boys were watching television. "Daddy!" the boys chimed in.

Susan turned as her sons sang out. "Oh, Bill..." She started to cry.

"Easy, sweetheart, I'm here now. Are you OK?" Susan kissed his mouth and buried her head tighter into his chest as she started to sob.

"Hi, sweet-pea. How's my little girl?" Adrian had a big smile on her face and looked like she had just woken from a nap.

"It was a miracle, Bill. Plain and simple, a miracle. There is no other way to describe it. It was a miracle…" Bill looked at the boys.

"How are you two guys doing?" Bill continued to hold Susan tightly and she wrapped her arms around his neck.

"We're sore. Our chest and neck hurts," both boys said together.

"But you guys are OK? Legs and arms, fingers and toes, smiles still working?" Both boys smiled and tried to get out of bed.

Nurse O'Neal moved toward them. "You two, stay put. I'm going to get your chocolate ice cream right now. Don't you move." Nurse O'Neal pointed her finger at them and left the room.

"Let me see Adrian." Bill freed one arm and moved to the side of his daughter's bed. Susan still clung to his left side and had both arms wrapped around his waist.

"How are your fingers and toes, little one? It looks like you're all here. Any hurts you want Daddy to kiss and make better?"

"No, Daddy, I feel fine. Mommy is the one that keeps crying."

Susan held Bill. "I'm telling you, Bill, it was a miracle. This total stranger comes out of nowhere and picks Adrian out of my lap and brings her back to life."

"That's what you said on the phone, sweetheart. I am sure there is a logical explanation for what happened. I am just glad you are all safe now. It looks like everyone is going to be fine." Nurse O'Neal bounded through the door.

"They're more than fine, Mr. Larkin, they were blessed. Believe me I know all about God blessing little ones. I have been a nurse in this hospital for twenty-four years and I have seen miracles before, yes siree. True there are cases where miracles don't happen, but this one was one of those exceptions." Nurse O'Neal stopped long enough to take a breath.

"Thank you for all of your help, Nurse. I can see you are a true professional and my family and I appreciate it very much." Bill Larkin was changing the subject, gently. "Do you suppose you could introduce me to the doctor responsible for the release of my family?"

"Sure, Mr. Larkin, I'll go and find him right away. But I don't think anyone is going home tonight."

"Oh no," the boys protested. "You mean we can't go home?"

"We'll let the doctor decide which of you gets to go home and when. We don't want to take any chances. Besides—"

Bill was cut off by Nurse O'Neil again. "Besides, your little sister is blessed and there are a lot of people waiting to see her out in the main lobby."

Bill's face reddened and he turned toward the door. "What do you mean there are a lot of people waiting to see 'her'? You mean there are reporters in the hospital wanting to interview my daughter about the accident?"

"Yes, sir, the lobby is full of them. The doctor told them to wait there until your wife and daughter were recovered enough to answer questions."

"Nurse, find the doctor now. I mean it, now." Bill Larkin was not about to have his family paraded in front of every nightly news crew in Los Angeles.

"Bill, don't be so harsh." Susan looked disappointed. "The nurse sees what has happened here and so does the doctor. More importantly so do I and I think it's important to tell the story."

"What story? That God came to Los Angeles today and stopped off at the I-5 to save a little girl? You want that all over the eleven o'clock news and on the headline of every paper in the country tomorrow morning? Susan, this is my business and I will not have you or Adrian subjected to the media for a story that may have a very simple explanation. We will have every crack pot in the city trying to claim a miracle child is living among us and they'll line up on our front lawn trying to have her bless them. There will be no interview and that is final."

"How do you know that what happened today wasn't a miracle? You weren't there, I was. I saw it all. I was part of it and so was Adrian. Without it we wouldn't be now discussing anything except, a funeral. Bill I—"

"Susan, trust me on this. We need to leave here without anyone jumping to any conclusions. I promise you I will investigate the entire incident before I pass judgment on whether or not this was a miracle. But until then there will be no interviews, no phone calls about the situation and no communication about what happened today except between us, in the privacy of our own home. Is that understood?"

"You're serious about this, aren't you?" Susan moved to him, placing both hands on his arms and looking intently at his expression.

"Are you trying to keep this story solely for your news crew?"

"Susan, if my news people are involved, and by now I am sure they are, they're just figuring out that this is about the Bill and Susan Larkin family. I have no intention of trying to make a scoop out of this and yes, I am definitely serious about keeping this quiet, until I can do some investigating on my own. You have no idea how this situation could turn into a circus even before tomorrow morning. Trust me on this.

"Do you all understand? This goes for everyone in the family. Nobody talks about it but me and I will tell you everything I find out. Agreed?" Everyone nodded and looked away. No one in the Larkin family had seen Bill this serious since the Rodney King farce. The trial and riots in Los Angeles had made him question not only the system but how low our civilization had fallen.

"Mr. Larkin, I'm Dr. Washington. I was on call when your family was brought into the emergency room. I called your family physician, Dr. Lewis. He asked me to have you call him as soon as we have spoken. I can see no reason for an extended stay in the hospital. Physically everyone is fine. Emotionally may be another matter, but that's not my field.

"I believe Dr. Lewis is going to cover some information regarding counseling. I have read and reread the reports from the paramedics and highway patrol officers on the scene. I was not there. That being the case, I have no opinion or even personal experience with such a phenomenon. I can only say that current tests, and I mean every test imaginable, show your daughter to be perfectly well and able to leave the hospital. Your wife and sons have bruises and they will be sore for a while.

"There is no physical trauma that can be treated. Other than a hot meal and a good night's rest, I can see no other recommendation. Blood pressures are a little higher than normal; however, considering the circumstances, I don't know what else can be done. Their blood pressures should be normal by morning. I will mention it to Dr. Lewis and have him check them again when he sees you later this evening."

"Thank you, Doctor. Do you need any information regarding insurance or how to reach us?" Bill placed his hand in Susan's.

"No, your wife had about everything we needed. Dr. Lewis filled in the rest. I suggest you call him before you leave the hospital. If you would like to use my office, you are more than welcome."

"Yes, please, Doctor. Susan, kids, please get your things together and be ready to leave when I come back." Bill was calm and in charge.

Dr. Washington walked toward the door. "Nurse, would you please help Mrs. Larkin with her children. You do want to leave as quietly as possible, correct, Mr. Larkin? There must be two dozen reporters with cameras, lights and satellite trucks in front of the hospital. I suggested a news conference would be forthcoming, as a distraction. You should be able to exit through our basement emergency access."

"Yes, Dr. Washington, we would prefer that to the alternative. Thank you."

Bill turned to his family. "Everyone, get ready now and remember, no reporters, no statements. Stay here until I come back for you. Susan?"

Susan looked at him with a helpless stare, tears still wetting her cheeks. "Hurry, Bill, please? I just want to get home." Susan started to help Adrian get dressed.

"I'll hurry." Dr. Washington led him down the hall to the elevator and up two floors, then to his office.

"Let me grab this clipboard and I will leave you alone. Dial 9 to reach an outside line then dial the number. The area code is the same."

"Again, Doctor, thank you for all your help. You are a true professional. I mean that." Bill picked up the receiver and dialed.

"Dr. Lewis please, this is Bill Larkin."

"Just a moment, the doctor is with a patient but he is expecting your call. I'll go get him."

"Bill, you there?" Bill Larkin had leaned back in the chair and held the receiver away from his ear to avoid the on hold music. He was deep in thought.

"Bill, are you there?"

"Yeah, Doc. I'm here."

"I spoke with Susan earlier. The story she told me was, well rather unbelievable. Have you had a chance to talk to her?"

Bill glanced around the room. "Not really. She says she witnessed a miracle. There are reporters lining up in front of the hospital. The doctor has given his OK for us to leave. He said you wanted to talk to me first."

"Yes, I think you should avoid going to the house. Susan needs to be with her parents and it would probably give you all time to settle. I want to give you the phone number of a colleague of mine, Dr. Will Hanson. He's a counselor, a psychologist really. He will be able to answer some questions and prescribe follow-up counseling."

"Do you think this is necessary?" Bill asked.

"Perhaps not. Just a precaution in case emotions run away. Better still, why don't you call me when you arrive at Susan's parents. She has already spoken with Jack and they are expecting you. I will come by and see everyone as soon as I am through here. I'll give you the phone number for Dr. Hanson when I see you. Are you all right?"

"Yeah sure. I don't really know what to think at this point. I'll see you later." Bill was distracted by a copy of the police and paramedic report lying on Dr. Washington's desk.

"Bill, are you sure you're OK?"

"Hell, Barney, I wasn't in the accident for Christ's sake. I'll call you from the Swansons'."

Bill started reading the report, then realized the family would be ready to go. The sooner the better. Anything to avoid the press. He took the report and folded it into his coat pocket. *For 'Christ's sake!'* he thought to himself.

Susan's father lived in Brentwood north of Sunset Boulevard on one of the full acre properties left over from the forties. Her dad had been a builder and got the old place for next to nothing. Several years and a few hundred thousand dollars later, he and Elaine, Susan's stepmother since early childhood, had a place even the very wealthy envied. It was secluded and would be the perfect place to hide and regain some normality. Susan's stepmother was standing in the open front door when they arrived.

"Elaine, we appreciate this on such short notice."

Before she could answer, a voice came from somewhere in the house. "Billy, is that you? Are Susan and the kids with you?" Susan's dad was calling from one of the side bedrooms.

"Yes, Jack, it's us." Bill gave Elaine a kiss on the cheek and rolled his eyes. Susan's dad was anything but a patient man. His heart was bigger than the state of California and gave him a lot of room to be himself. Bill's arms were full of Quicksilver bags. Ken Taylor had retrieved them from the wrecked van and dropped them off at the hospital. Bill could avoid going by the house for several days thanks to a good cop and thoughtful friend.

"Here, let me at some of that stuff, Billy. You go help Adrian." Jack took the bags.

"We're right here, Dad." Susan followed Bill into the entry way.

Jack dropped the bags. "My girls. My beautiful girls. Thank God you're all right."

The boys came in next. "Grandpa."

Jack had already kissed Susan, hugged Bill and was holding Adrian. "How are my favorite cowboys? Come in the kitchen. Grandpa has a big pot of spaghetti and meatballs, a chocolate cake and lots of ice cream." Jack turned toward the kitchen leaving the bags on the hall floor.

Bill smiled as he bent over to pick up the bags. "You all go ahead. I'll get the luggage and put everything in the bedrooms. I'll just be a minute."

Susan wrapped her arms around Bill's neck tightly, he dropped the bags and put his arms around her waist. Elaine smiled and turned toward the kitchen.

"I love it when he calls you Billy. You know, sweetheart, it was a miracle. I was there. He asked me if I believed and I said I did. Adrian came back to life in his arms. Bill, I swear. I was there I saw her I was holding her—"

"Susan, darling, I believe you. Just hold me. Shhhhhhh," he whispered in her ear. "I am proud of you, Susan. You knew exactly what to do. You saved Adrian's life."

Susan started to cry again. "It was the stranger. I was helpless," Susan whispered back.

Bill had tears on his cheeks. "I know, sweetheart, I know. Come on in the kitchen. I'll fix us a drink as soon as I finish with the gear." Bill took her arms from around his neck and led her into the kitchen.

Jack looked up from the spaghetti pot. "Susan, come here and give the old man a kiss." Susan let go of Bill's hand and went to her father.

Bill retrieved the bags and overnight kits and placed them in the guest rooms. The house was so big ten guests could comfortably stay in seclusion hardly seeing one another for a week.

Susan was an only child but Jack Swanson had a million friends. His first wife died not long after Susan's third birthday. She was killed in a skiing accident at June Lake. Until Elaine came along two years later, Jack had all but given up on life. During those two years, Susan spent most of her time with her aunt and uncle, Wally and Anita Wilkens. Anita was Jack's sister and Wally was a highway patrol officer.

Bill carried in the last of the bags and closed the door behind him. In the larger of the five guest rooms, the one he and Susan had shared since their honeymoon, he took off his coat. He picked up the phone to dial Dr. Lewis and noticed the accident report in the pocket of his jacket. He read it over quickly, struggling with the handwriting and abbreviations as Ken Taylor had filled it out. He read it slower a second time and the impact of what had happened began to sink in. Although Kenny did not come right out and say he witnessed a miracle, it was obvious that something extraordinary had happened. The paramedic report was more direct.

> In all of my previous experience as an emergency medical technician, I have never seen a person brought back to life without the aid of medical equipment. As far as I saw, it was a miracle-medical, spiritual, whatever. It was a miracle.

Bill folded the report and returned it to his pocket. He picked up the receiver and dialed Dr. Lewis.

"Barney, we're here. Everyone is eating Jack's famous spaghetti. Maybe you should come by in the morning."

"My schedule is packed tomorrow. I would feel better if I saw Susan, Adrian, and the boys tonight. Will Jack mind?" Dr. Lewis knew Jack would be glad he came.

"I'm sure he won't. You had better bring an appetite. I am sure Susan will feel better after your visit. How long have you been her doctor? Something like 30 years?"

"Thirty-four to be exact. I cared for her when she was staying with Anita and Uncle Wally. Wally and I went to high school together. Did you call Anita yet?"

"No, but I'm sure Jack did. I'll see you when you get here. Drive carefully, Doc." Bill sat on the edge of the bed for a moment, thinking.

"A miracle, huh? Could the world handle a miracle? It sure as hell could use one." Bill picked up his jacket and walked to the kitchen. Everyone was eating except Jack.

"You know I've read about these healers in the jungles of South America. Do you suppose it was one of those guys?" Jack spoke with excitement.

Bill sighed. "I suggest we not speculate. I for one am grateful you are all here and you are all safe. I don't know what to think of the events or the course they took today. If it was a miracle, then I thank God. If it wasn't, well everything happens for a reason." Bill put his arm around Susan.

Jack raised his arms. "Amen to that, Billy."

Susan looked into Bill's eyes. "It was a miracle." Tears started to flow again.

"Dr. Lewis is on his way over just to check on everybody. Jack, I told him to bring his feed bag. He said he was starving for some of your famous meatballs."

"And amen to that too," yelled Jack.

"I left my car at the hospital. In our haste to escape the press I left my suitcase and travel bag in the trunk."

"I've got plenty of stuff here, Billy boy, you don't need to drive over to the hospital again tonight." Jack moved around the counter heading for his bedroom.

"To be honest, I may have left my car unlocked. I would rest better knowing it was secure."

Jack stopped in his tracks just as he was stripping off his apron. "I can understand that, boy. I'll grab my coat and go with you."

"Really, dear, Susan and the children need you here and Dr. Lewis is on his way. Let Bill go by himself." Elaine was a lifesaver.

"She's right, Jack. I'll only be gone a while and it wouldn't be right for you to leave now."

"OK, OK, I know when I'm needed elsewhere. You get going and get back here safe." Jack retied his apron and moved back behind his pot.

Bill took Susan's hand and helped her up from her chair. "Will you be fine if I leave? I'll stay if you want."

Susan smiled. "No, we'll be fine." She hugged him and kissed him on the mouth. Then she whispered in his ear, "You're going to the station, aren't you? Do you think you can find the stranger?"

Bill stood back. She knew him better than he knew himself.

"Adrian, guys, you OK if Daddy leaves for a while?" He knew they were in great hands and Susan was right. He was going to the station.

"We're fine, Daddy. Grandpa has a new video and there is still cake and ice cream."

Adrian didn't say anything. She got off her chair and walked over to her father. "Daddy? You be careful. Do you think you can find the stranger?"

Bill blinked back the tears. "You get a good night's sleep, baby girl." He picked her up and kissed her. "Daddy will take care of everything."

"I'll see you all later." He let go of Susan's arm, then returned for one more kiss.

Chapter 3
The City of Angels

IN LESS THAN ONE month, the dedication of the Thomas B. Rich Museum of Modern Art was going to take place on the top of a man-made mountain. The view from the main terrace overlooked the Santa Monica shoreline and Century City. At the museum entrance, a plaque designed by the man responsible for the vast sum of money donated to its construction and furnishing was being installed under a life-size statue in his likeness. The plaque read:

Man has always possessed a great desire to trail the sun west. Even the sure knowledge of death, by falling off the edge of the world, would not dissuade him. Once on the North American continent man pressed on, driving the Native Americans before him. Pushing across the plains, over the great Rockies, discovering the beauty of the great Northwest as it plunged into the blue Pacific.

From there man marched south, seeking a warmer climate, driven by tales of a wondrous land in an endless basin, surrounded by mountains converging with the sea.

Today, men and women from every geographical location in the world vie for a piece of Southern California. In a never-ending movement of mankind in search of riches, a better life, the sun, or a place in the Hollywood myth. Ultimately they will all rest here at my feet, in the City of Angels.

Thomas B. Rich January 1, 2000.

"Mr. Rich, isn't that statement slightly arrogant?" The question asked by Jane Turner of KBLA news of Los Angeles. There were no cameras, no lights, and no one else sitting on the terrace except Mr. Thomas B. Rich and Jane Turner.

"No, I don't think it is arrogant at all. I built this museum and most of the view you see before you. Eventually everyone coming to Los Angeles will visit my museum and certainly they will wind up standing right where you are now. At my feet." Thomas Rich smiled his controlling smile.

"I understand my boss's wife works for you as an art curator. Is that correct?" Jane was trying to get him on a subject other than himself.

"Who, Susan Larkin? She's a fine piece of…womanhood." Thomas caught himself. "I usually don't go for the married mother type, but I might make an exception in her case."

"I'm sure Bill Larkin will be happy to hear that. He is my boss you know."

"Yes, yes I know and I am sure he would love to hear all about how far back we go, wouldn't he, Janie?" Thomas was always one step ahead.

"It's a small world, isn't it, Mr. Rich?" Jane smiled as Thomas shifted gears.

"You see, Jane, Los Angeles was founded so I could be where I am today. During the Spanish conquests and then for the next one hundred years, the best land was divided into land grants, and given to those in favor of the Spanish court. But land alone did not bring prosperity to Southern California. It was the stuff that lay beneath the surface of the land and Thomas Rich that made Los Angeles the city it is today."

Jane settled in for what was to be a preliminary meeting for a story KBLA was going to do on the life of Thomas B. Rich and Rich Industries. The one-hour special would air prior to the opening of the Rich Museum.

Thomas continued. "One of the greatest stories ever told, traveled on the lips of the rich and those that dreamed of being rich, about the man, John Davison Rockefeller. The year was 1860 John D. was 20 years old and a partner in a produce firm named after him and his partner, Clark & Rockefeller. John D. was sent on an investigative assignment to Titusville, Pennsylvania, about 100 miles away from Cleveland, Ohio, where he and Maurice Clark prospered in the produce business during the War Between the States.

"Am I going to fast for you, Jane?" Thomas sat down in the other Victorian chair and picked up a glass of his favorite brandy sitting on an 18th-century table standing between the two chairs.

The area was screened off and the chairs were facing the ocean. It was all arranged to show the power behind the man. Jane declined Thomas's offer of her own glass of liquor. Then he continued.

"John D.'s mission for the Cleveland Produce commission was to find out if there was any future in the oil business. His report, 'Petroleum has no future.' He and Clark invested $4,000 of their combined savings into Samuel Andrews lard refinery in Cleveland. Two years later John D. paid $75,000 to Maurice Clark for his interest in the Samuel Andrews lard/oil refinery and went into the oil business. Three years later at the age of 25, John D. Rockefeller and his new partner, Samuel Andrews, were producing more than 500 barrels of oil a day, realizing by year's end, a gross of more than $1,000,000."

Jane had stopped writing notes and sipped at a glass of water.

"In the spring of 1879 the Pacific Coast Oil Company opened a new refinery in San Francisco, California, with four oil wells to feed the refinery and all of the processed crude going to John D's Standard Oil Company. Thus began one of the great American success stories. Men lived and died with the dream to become the next John D. Rockefeller. Few men made it, most died. Men and money have a way of changing the world for better and for worse, don't you think, Jane?"

Thomas stood and walked to the handcrafted marble railing. On the other side of the railing was an 80-foot drop-off giving the impression that as one stood safely on the terrace, one could fly. Thomas did not wait for an answer from the reporter.

"Oil was discovered in Los Angeles at the same time the railroads arrived, between 1870 and 1890. Oil was the substance that put Los Angeles on the map and turned big business toward Los Angeles Harbor. But the real strike in the Southern California area came in 1920, when black gold was discovered in Long Beach where the sun met the sand."

Thomas turned to face Jane Turner. She was not writing any notes and she had not brought a tape recorder at the insistence of Mr. Rich. Thomas grew sullen.

"A young unwed girl named Melissa Thomas gave birth to a son on a cot in one of the railroad camps. She wasn't sure who the father was so she gave him her last name as his first, Thomas. She made Boy as his middle name, since he was a boy and Rich his last because she wanted to be. That's right; I was born in a tent. The floor was black from the soil that oozed up through the canvas bottom. I'm sure I sucked hard on my mama's breast because it tasted sweet and warm in my mouth and I wanted it all." Thomas smiled his seductive smile.

"I grew up hating the railroad workers for taking turns with my mother inside our tent. When I was eight, I packed my clothes in a small burlap sack where I kept some meager personal items and left her. Walking down Ocean Avenue toward the rail head of the Red Car Line, I saw a man in a suit telling some other men to get back to work."

He had Jane's attention now. She was listening to every word.

"The man was yelling, 'I told you men for the last time. Pick up your tools and fix this broken track.'

"But they yelled back. 'Mr. Andersen, for the last time we ain't going to work on Sunday for regular wages. Every time you have a broken rail you drag us out on our day off and pay us standard pay.' The six men standing before Mr. Andersen were big burly railroad men the kind I had grown up hating. One of the men grabbed a pick handle and started toward Mr. Andersen."

Thomas turned to the railing and gripped it with both hands. Jane picked up her pen and pad.

"Go on, Mr. Rich." She started writing again.

"They told Andersen they were through talking. They said, 'Either you pay us double or we're gonna split your head open right here on these tracks.' The man raised the handle ready to strike.

"That's when I stepped up. 'Hey, mister, I know you. You been in my tent with my mama and I know your face.' I stood in front of Mr. Andersen. 'If you hit this man I'll tell the police it was you who done it.' Then I doubled up my fists and dug in my feet.

"One of them hollered, 'Don't let that kid stop you, Charlie, hit the son of a bitch in the head.' But the man with the pick handle stopped and stared at me. He said, 'I can't hit no kid.' He stood there for a long few minutes then he repeated himself. 'I can't hit no kid.' In spite of the prodding of his comrades, he dropped the pick handle and walked away. One of the other men pointed a finger in Andersen's face and spit.

"'You ain't heard the last of us, Samuel Andersen. We startin' a union and you will do what we say or you'll have no workers. That's a promise.' With that the other five men spit on the ground right at my and Mr. Andersen's feet. Then they walked away swearing.

"'That was a brave thing to do for such a young boy,' Mr. Andersen said."

Jane stood and walked to the railing.

"I told Mr. Andersen how I felt, 'Mr. Andersen, I hate those bastards.' Then I spit after them. That was the first time I remember getting a good look at Mr. Andersen's face. It was red from the sun and his round rimmed glasses made his face look even rounder. He put his hand on my head and messed my hair.

"'That is no way for a boy your size to talk. What is your name?' he asked.

"'Thomas Boy Rich, sir,' I said."

Mr. Andersen continued. "'Well, Thomas Boy Rich, thank you for saving my life. I'm not afraid of a fight, I've been in plenty. But six against one is pretty tough odds even for an old railroad man like me.' He told me his name was Samuel H. Andersen as his face broke into a smile." Thomas's voice had gotten softer and distant.

"'What are you doing up town this time of day? Shouldn't you be in church?' he bellowed at me. I told him I didn't go to school or church."

Thomas walked back to the table and took another drink of brandy, pouring a glass for Jane, despite the fact she had declined earlier. "He asked me how old I was. I told him I was eight, almost nine."

"Didn't he ask you about your parents?" Jane took the glass and turned a page continuing to write.

"Yes, he asked me if I lived in one of the tents. He heard me mention it when I was talking to the railroad men. He asked me if I lived in the 'Railroad Camp.'"

"What did you say?" Thomas had slowed his speech and was deep into his childhood. Jane was baiting him to continue.

Thomas took a deep breath and talked in the voice of a child. "'I did but I don't live there anymore. And I don't have any folks. Just my mama and she's a whore.'" Thomas turned to look at Jane. As an eight-year-old boy he had never said the word whore before even though he had heard it plenty of times yelled by the men in the camp when they wouldn't pay his mother.

"Older kids in the camp told me what a whore was," Thomas explained as his eyes filled with tears and as they did he turned away and looked toward the city.

"I told Mr. Andersen I wasn't going back to the camp ever again. I told him I hated railroad men and I hated the railroad. But he just smiled his big red-faced smile at me.

"'Well, son, you just saved an old railroad man from getting his head split open.'

"I told him he didn't look like a railroad man all dressed up in a suit and all.

"He said, 'I don't build the railroad with my hands anymore. I'm the engineer and construction manager for the Red Car Line. I work for Mr. Henry Huntington.'

"Then Samuel Andersen picked up my sack and reached out to take my hand. 'Let's go have a talk with your mother,' he said.

"Samuel had seen more than his share of rail line prostitutes in all of his years around the camps. They were usually illiterate and sickly—my mother was neither.

"'Miss Thomas, my name is Samuel Andersen,' he spoke to her from outside the tent in case she was not alone.

"She yelled back at him, 'I don't need any names, mister, and I'm not working today, it's Sunday. So whoever you are come back tomorrow.'"

Jane turned another page and took a sip of brandy. Thomas took a large swallow of his as he returned to his chair. Then after a long pause he continued.

"'Miss Thomas it's not like that. I found your son walking down by the rail line in town. He said he was running away. I have com to return him. May we come in?' Samuel was always the gentleman. My mother stuck her head out of the tent.

"'Tommy ain't missin'. He's just off with some of his kid friends.' She was wearing a white slip and no shoes. The tent opening split where her shoulder parted it so her head could stick out. Her slip was clean and sheer. Her right breast was faintly visible through the white cotton lace that made up the V-cut neckline. She looked first at Andersen, then at me. I looked away so I couldn't see her face.

33

"'Tommy, is this man tellin' the truth? Were you downtown?' I couldn't speak. I just continued to look away. For the first time I realized what my mother really was.

"Samuel spoke first. 'Please, Miss Thomas, may we step inside?' Samuel Andersen was in his early fifties, tall, with a muscular build growing slowly toward his waistline. He was powerful, a real leader.

"Mother answered him. 'Yes of course. Let me put on a robe or something.' Her head and shoulder slipped back inside the tent. A few seconds later she invited him in.

"The tent was larger than the usual camp tent. It had a pull drape across the middle and a spacious back section with a large bed built out of fine timber and a feather mattress. There was a cherrywood chest of drawers and a mirror attached to a large wooden stand. The stand served as a clothes rack as well. There was a small worn sofa in the front part of the tent. I slept in a handmade single bed on apple crates held together by boards and nails with a small mattress, with some worn sheets and a blanket. Both ends of the tent had a flap allowing men to come and go from the main bedroom without coming into the area where I slept.

"It's funny, I haven't thought about this in a long time but, it seems like it was yesterday."

Jane reached out and touched his arm. He had become so childlike. So openly vulnerable. Thomas poured more brandy into his glass as he continued.

"Mother went on, 'Sit down, Mr. Andersen. Tommy, what does he mean you were running away?' I looked at the ground and moved the black earth with the toe of my boot.

"'Miss Thomas, I'm not sure what is going on here but your son is upset about your living conditions. He—' Mr. Andersen was coming to my rescue. Mama wouldn't stand for his inference.

"'Our living conditions. What business is that of yours, Mr. Andersen or whoever in the hell you think you are. Are you some kind of priest?'

"He responded, 'No, I'm with the railroad—'

"But Mama was mad as a fighting rooster. 'And I suppose you have a big fancy house up on the Boulevard and grass and roses and a wife cooking in a big kitchen and well dressed little kiddies running up and down the stairs. Am I right so far, Mr. Railroad man?' I was embarrassed for her talking like that to a fine gentleman. But it didn't stop Samuel.

"'No, not exactly. I have a home on Wilshire and a wife but we were never able to have children. That is not why I am here, Miss Thomas. I want to talk about your son. He told me he is not in school and that he thinks all railroad men are bastards.'

"'Well he's not far wrong, is he, Mr. Railroad man,' Mama replied.

"'I work for the railroad, that's true but my area of expertise is in the public sector, building the Red Car Line. Your son is almost nine, is that correct?' Samuel just wouldn't give up." Thomas smiled and drank again.

"Mama was just getting madder. I thought she was going to throw something at him, but she just yelled, 'Yeah, so what? Look, what do you want from us? Just make your point and get out!'

"'I want to help. Your son stood between me and a man that was going to bash my brains in this afternoon. I can't remember the last time I saw that much bravery in anyone, let alone a nine-year-old boy. He knew the man from his visits to you in your tent. Then he told me he was running away. I wanted to offer my help if there is anything you will accept from me.'

"Mama was shocked. 'Tommy, you did that? You saved this man?' I nodded.

"'I can tell your son is a smart boy. He speaks better than most kids I know, even the ones older than he is.' Samuel put his hand on my shoulder and squeezed his strong right hand into my coat.

"'Mama taught me how to read and write too, Mr. Andersen. She's real smart,' I blurted out." His voice was again that of a little boy.

Jane was curiously drawn to his vulnerability. She placed her pad and pen on the table and reached out for Thomas's hand. Thomas spoke on.

"'You're an educated woman, Miss Thomas?' Samuel asked.

"Mama resented his question. 'Why? Would that surprise you, Mr. Andersen?' She turned her back and acted suddenly like a prep schoolgirl.

"'Yes, sir. I went to school in Boston until my daddy moved us to San Francisco so he could work for the Standard Oil Company. He was killed in a refinery explosion and my mother went crazy. She's in a hospital in Oakland, for insane people. I came down here with a man I met. He was working for the Southern Pacific Railroad.

"'When he found out I was pregnant and I had been sleeping with this other man, besides him, he killed the other fella and disappeared. He said we were going to get married but I don't think he would have unless I was pregnant. The other fella said he would marry me for sure. I was broke. Then other men started coming around offering me money to sleep with them. I never finished high school but I got through the eleventh grade. I have been teaching Tommy how to read and write, and speak well too.'"

Thomas squeezed Jane's hand. "Mama was a proud woman in spite of her circumstances.

"Samuel spoke respectfully to her. 'I can see you are doing the best you can. I would like to see Thomas in school. I will help you find a worthy job and an apartment if you'll let me. Right now though I have a rail line to repair before the first line goes out in the morning. Will you allow me to come back tomorrow so we can discuss this further? You think about it tonight and maybe the two of you can come up with what you

36

want for each other. Is tomorrow all right for you then?'"

Thomas let go of Jane's hand and took another drink. "Samuel was the first sincere person I'd ever met and the only man I have ever trusted."

Thomas sank deeper in his chair and went on with his story. First quoting his mother. "'Yes, sir, it's OK with me. Is it OK, Tommy?' I nodded and shook hands with Samuel. He offered to send us some protection until the following day. Mama turned him down. He turned to leave. I thought I would never see him again. Then he bent down so he could look me directly in the eyes.

"'You can wait another day before you have to run away, right, son?' I gave him a quick smile and put on my cap. 'That's a good lad then. Thanks again for saving my life.' Samuel Andersen left the tent and walked back to the rail head on Ocean Avenue. He told me later he couldn't get over how brave I had been. He felt something special about me and made a vow to himself to do everything he could to help me, his little savior and my mama." Thomas started to choke up like his throat was constricting.

"That night, two hours after midnight, three men came into the tent. They whispered threats to Mama about me and my big mouth as well as how she was no more than a filthy whore and had no business with a son in her tent anyway. Each man had a club and started beating Mama beneath her covers. I rolled off my bed and under the crate frame just as a club crashed through the wood sending splinters down over my neck and head. Several more blasts came as the wood frame broke down under the tremendous blows from the pick handle clubs. One blow glanced off a broken piece of wood and split the crown of my head, knocking me unconscious. That was the last thing I remembered until the next morning when Mr. Andersen stood next to me along with a doctor bandaging my head. I struggled to get up.

"'Where's Mama? Mr. Andersen, where is my mama?' I

tried to stand but fell back against the doctor's chest.

"'Your mother didn't make it, Thomas. She was alive when I arrived here this morning but before the doctor could get here, she died. I'm sorry, son. Before she died though she asked me to take care of you. I promised her I would. With her last breath she said, "Tell Thomas Boy, I love him," and then she passed on, son. I am terribly sorry. I promise you we will find the men that did this. I promise you that, son.'

"I could barely speak but I managed to say, 'Those dirty railroad bastards. I'll kill every last one of them.' Then I slipped back into unconsciousness. The next time I awoke was in my new home with Samuel and Elizabeth Andersen. Out of respect for Mama I never changed my name."

Thomas put his glass on the table and looked at Jane Turner. She was kneeling next to him holding his hand. Her cheeks were wet with tears. Thomas stiffened, his eyes began to look like gathering storm clouds as he thrust her hand away.

"Wipe your tears, whore, and go back to your fucking news station." Thomas pulled his hand away and walked back into the museum.

Chapter 4
How Thomas Boy Got Rich

THOMAS LEFT THE MUSEUM and drove north along Pacific Coast Highway toward Malibu. He activated the electronic gate from a remote control button attached above his dashboard. The driveway was steep as it ascended down to the beach and into his private garage at the base of a three-story waterfront beach home. It was his hideaway. Not that no one knew it existed, but when Thomas wanted to be alone he came here. Everyone that needed to know knew not to disturb him under any circumstances while he was at the beach.

Thomas changed his clothes and fixed a drink. He looked out to the ocean and noticed a beautiful sunny afternoon in spite of the winter season. He thought, *God I love California.*

After his second drink, Thomas walked down to the water and started walking north toward the top of the cove. His thoughts returned to his past. Samuel and Elizabeth Andersen were swirling in his head like it was yesterday. When he reached the rocks, he found a large flat bolder still warm from the afternoon sun. He stretched out and started to daydream. Back to his childhood and the tragic end of Samuel and Elizabeth Andersen.

The Andersens became the perfect parents for Thomas Boy, as Elizabeth Andersen chose to call him. She called him

Tommy once, as he remembered and he made no bones about the fact that no one called him 'Tommy.'

Samuel continued on with the Red Car Line as president and general manager of the Long Beach based operation. Thomas dreamed of the times when Samuel explained to him about his investments and how, during the years of construction, Samuel Andersen had taken his bonus money and the proceeds from his oil investments in Standard Oil and purchased land along the waterfront and adjacent to the harbor in Long Beach. He often spoke of how the oil business continued to bring prosperity to all of those having the foresight and financial ability to get in at the right time. Samuel Andersen had become a rich man. Not only by purchasing land that was soon wanted by the oil companies moving into the oil rich area, but he had maintained the mineral rights as well. Texaco, Standard Oil, Shell, Unocal and others all wanted to lease, drill and pipe on the Andersen lands. Thomas thought of his great success and silently thanked the man whose forethought made it all possible.

He remembered how after his ninth birthday and the death of his mother, the Andersens took legal custody of the young man who had saved Samuel on the Red Car tracks. He grew up privileged. He recalled his enrollment in private schools and how he graduated from grade 12 by the time he was 15. Like Samuel, his interests were in the oil business. So much so, he would rather go to the office with Samuel than play school games with classmates. Thomas remembered his 16th birthday. That was the same year he entered Pepperdine College, a newly created center of advanced education founded in Los Angeles, as the youngest and ultimately the richest alumnus ever to attend Pepperdine University.

Thomas relished the thoughts of how he spent every minute studying the history of business. His idols became John D. Rockefeller, William Randolph Hearst, and Henry Ford. From school each afternoon until Friday when he went to Samuel's Long Beach office for lunch, then home for the weekend, he would walk to the main library in downtown Los Angeles. He was there when his roommate and best friend, Larry Dawkins, found him on a Wednesday evening in May 1946.

"Thomas, thank God you are still here. Someone from your house has been calling the school looking for you. They say it's an emergency and that you should call as soon as you get word." Without speaking Thomas stood and went to the front desk.

"I need to use a telephone. There is some urgent matter at my home and I must make a call immediately." Thomas was calm. His strong build and six-foot-four-inch frame commanded a presence that always got results.

"Yes, Mr. Rich, come into my office—here behind the counter." He followed the librarian into the office.

"You can have privacy in here." The head librarian knew Thomas well. Since his first days at Pepperdine he had made the library his home away from home. Reading, studying and asking for books not currently found on the shelves.

Thomas closed the door behind the exiting librarian and sat behind the desk. He dialed the number. The phone rang several times and was answered by Samuel's attorney, Edgar Jamison.

"Edgar, this is Thomas, I was told to call as soon as I was notified."

"Thomas, it's Samuel and Elizabeth." Edgar's voice quivered.

"They're in New York for an oil convention and fundraiser for the Rockefeller Foundation. Is there a problem?" Thomas spoke quickly.

"They were going to San Francisco on a special Eastern Airline flight provided by Laurence Rockefeller. Everyone on board had been attending the convention and decided to come to the West Coast for a big celebration. It was to be a gift for all of the large contributors. Thomas, the plane crashed. There were no survivors."

"I'm coming home." Thomas put down the receiver and

covered his face with both hands. There was no one looking but he refused to allow anyone see him with tears in his eyes. The tears came slowly and few in numbers. Except for recalling these memories it would be the last time Thomas B. Rich ever shed a tear for another human being.

Edgar Jamison came through the front door when he heard Thomas's car pull around the long circular drive. He stood on the porch with his hands crossed at his belt looking more like an undertaker than an attorney. Thomas never did see much difference between attorneys, vultures and undertakers.

"I am truly sorry for your loss, Thomas. Your father... I mean Samuel Andersen was more than a client. He was a dear friend."

"Cut the butter, Edgar. You needed Samuel more than he ever needed you. I want to see the will as soon as we get into the house. If there is anyone else named, I will personally see to it that they receive whatever Samuel designated."

"That's not how it works, Thomas, you know that better than anyone. First we must—"

"First we must agree on your final bill and I will give you a check as soon as I see the will. Otherwise you can leave now and never receive a dime from me or the estate. Do you understand me, lawyer?" Thomas gave him the look he had already become famous for among his peers. It was a look that contained a demand, hinging on your immediate correct decision to comply or you would think the hand of God had come down upon you for some unforgivable crime.

"Are we clear, Mr. Jamison? I do not repeat myself."

"Yes, Mr. Rich, perfectly clear. I will open the document at once and present you with my fee."

I, Samuel Hoarse Andersen, being of sound mind and judgment, before the witness Mr. Edgar Jamison, also my legal representative, bequeath the following: To my wife, Elizabeth Jean Andersen, I leave our home and one fourth of my estate at the time of my death. Should she survive beyond the amount indicated as one fourth of my estate, my son and heir apparent, Thomas Boy Rich, shall provide for her until her death. The remaining three fourths of my estate including all businesses, lands and holdings such as stocks, bonds and outstanding loans to the individuals mentioned herein shall become the property in total of my son, Thomas Boy Rich, legally adopted November 24, 1929.

Should the conditions be such that my wife and I meet death together, the entire estate shall go to Mr. Thomas Boy Rich. Signed on the March 17, 1938, my son's 18th birthday. Mr. Samuel H. Andersen

"The will was signed in my presence, as indicated, and notarized by me, Edgar Jamison, Esquire. My bill in the amount of $2,735 is for services rendered and clears your late father's current balance. Will there be anything else, Mr. Rich?" Jamison handed the papers to Thomas Boy.

"I see by Samuel's figures he loaned you $5,000 three years ago and I see nothing to indicate your repayment. Why is that, Mr. Jamison?"

"He loaned me the money for a down payment on a house. It is the home I live in with my family. He said I could pay him back when things improved. Your father was one of only five clients I have with the ability to pay their legal fees. Your father being by far the wealthiest of the five."

"I see. If my math is correct, and I assure you it is, to the penny, you owe me $2,265. However, I also notice the outstanding balance owed to you for legal services is $235. Please explain the other $2,500."

"The additional $2,500 is for exercising the will and—"

"Mr. Jamison, I hardly think the last fifteen minutes of your time is worth $2,500. Do you?"

"Mr. Rich, the estate you have just inherited is worth an estimated $25,000,000 and the estimate is conservative. I am only asking one tenth of one percent for the legal services rendered for the keeping and reading of the will. It is only ri—"

"Mr. Jamison, I have no intention to stand here and argue with you on my day of mourning. I will offer you no more than two hundred dollars for your services, leaving you in debt to me for $4,565 payable immediately or I will begin foreclosure on your property. That is my final decision."

"Mr. Rich, this is an outrage. I can no more come up with that kind of money than I could sprout wings and fly. I don't understand your thinking."

"My thinking is not for you to understand. I am a businessman and from this day forward I will make every decision based on the principal of sound business. Your services are no longer required by this company or family. Therefore, it is in my best interest to collect the outstanding debt and turn it into a credit. If you can't pay I promise you, I will take your house and property." Thomas slammed the will down hard on table in front of him.

"I'll need a day or two to see what I can collect or borrow to pay what I owe you. Please, Mr. Rich, consider my wife and children."

"Your wife and children do not enter into it. Samuel spoke well of you when he was alive, so out of respect for him I will give you until the day of the funeral. At that time I expect full payment or the deed to your home. Are we clear, Mr. Jamison?"

"Yes, sir, Mr. Rich, we are clear. I can see why you never took the name of your adopted parents. The blood in their veins was blue and warm, yours is black and cold as a blizzard."

"You had better leave before it freezes around your throat. I expect full payment three days from this afternoon. Now get out of my house!" Thomas stood behind the large black oak desk Samuel had purchased in Europe. It was 400 years old and had belonged to one of the oldest trading families in Germany. He sat down in the soft black, high backed leather chair just as he had seen Samuel do from the time he was a child. This is where he longed to be. At the threshold of one of the wealthiest oil fortunes in Los Angeles. He picked up the phone and dialed.

"Phi Beta. The house with a brain and women with big breasts."

"Get Larry Dawkins for me." Thomas was direct and demanding.

"Yeah, just a minute, your hind ass. I am at your serve ass." Everyone knew the voice of Thomas Boy Rich. The young genius from the Wilshire District. The rich kid everyone wanted to be like but nobody wanted to be him.

"This is Dawkins."

"Mr. Dawkins. How would you like a job?" Thomas smiled as he leaned back in his new high backed chair. He swung his feet up on the desk.

"Thomas, what happened? Is everything OK? I was waiting to hear from you. Is it true about the plane crash? It's on the radio, on every station."

"It is true. There were no survivors. Samuel and Elizabeth are dead."

"I'm sorry, Thomas. I know how much they both meant to you. Is there anything I can do?"

"Hell yes, you can do something. You can take the job I just offered you and start collecting $35,000 a year being my vice president in charge of acquisitions. You know more about real estate and real estate law than I will ever want to know. What do you say?"

"Are you serious? I have two more years of graduate school and—"

"Don't you understand, Dawkins? Schools over. Class is out for good. I just inherited $25,000,000, most of which is in real estate and I am offering you a chance of a lifetime."

"You inherited how much?"

"Roughly twenty-five million dollars and the house of course. Pack your bags and move in here with me for the time being. I want to get started running the business the way I have always dreamed and I want to start today. Isn't $35,000 enough for your eternal loyalty and the fact that you will never make this much out of college with all of the degrees in the world. How about $40,000?"

"Make it $45,000 and I am on my way." Larry Dawkins held his breath.

"Done. I was afraid I had chosen the wrong man for the job. I'll be here when you arrive. Listen, you son of a bitch, be ready to work when you get here. My idea of success is to own Los Angeles and everything that leads in and out of this city will be a part of that success. Are you still there? What are you waiting for?" Thomas Boy Rich hung up the phone and started looking for a mortuary. The funeral arrangements would be the first assignment of his new vice president.

Thomas awoke as a flock of seagulls, gnawing at the setting sun, flew overhead. He had dozed off for more than an hour. He stretched and smiled at the strength he had gained in his youth. Samuel would be proud, he thought.

Chapter 5
Chairman of the Board

THOMAS WENT BACK TO the beach house and stripped himself on the front porch before going in. He wanted to sit in the hot tub and relax before Crystal came to escort him to dinner.

He went up to the second deck and removed the cover, activating the bubbles with a timer switch. He climbed into the tub. As the hot water swirled around his chest and neck, he closed his eyes and leaned his head back against the cushion fixed to the side wall. He wasn't sure if it was the heat or the brandy, but his thoughts returned to his incredible ascent to being the most powerful man in the oil business. His thoughts were transported back to the day of Samuel and Elizabeth's funeral and the events leading up to his current position as chairman of the board.

"Larry, see to it the minister receives his fee and thank Samuel and Elizabeth's friends for coming to the services. I have business to settle with Edgar Jamison. Then have all of these flowers taken over to the whore house on Elm Street, you know the one. Tell Katie they're from me to the girls. I'll see you back at the house by 2:00 p.m. Any questions?"

"None, except, the whore house?" scratching his head with his hat in his hand.

"Yes. Mama would like that. Samuel and Elizabeth don't care. Now that I think about it though, the one large wreath that says 'Rest in Peace,' set it on the front steps of the Rail Workers Union Hall. Those stupid bastards might as well know the end is coming. It won't be long before I put them out of business for good." Thomas gave a half smile as he looked past Larry Dawkins at the waiting Jamison.

"Well, what are you waiting for, Mr. Dawkins? We have a meeting in less than two hours and I want you here on time."

"Yes, sir, Mr. President." With that Larry turned on his heels and gave directions for the gravediggers to place the flowers in the back of his car. He was driving a brand-new 1946 Black Packard. It was a signing bonus from his friend and employer, T. B. Rich. The new automobile, the three new tailored suits and twelve custom made shirts were part of the new Thomas B. Rich Corporation image, as Thomas told Larry. In fact it was payoff for lifetime loyalty and servitude. There wasn't anything Lawrence W. Dawkins would not do for his ex-college roommate and employer. At twenty-one years of age he had already prospered beyond his grandest dreams.

Thomas remembered his first act as the new boss of Wilshire Boulevard.

"Jamison, do you have my money?"

"Yes, Mr. Rich, it is all here. Fifteen hundred in cash and a bank draft for three thousand and sixty-five dollars. The bank draft is a loan on the little equity I had in the house. The cash is from a union boss. He makes loans using members' funds, at an interest rate more than three times that of the bank. It's robbery. But it means I don't owe you a damn penny after today. Our business is finished." Edgar turned to go. If his mouth wasn't so dry, he would have spit at Thomas's feet. But he had just completed the most difficult oration in his life.

"Edgar, I haven't dismissed you yet."

"I am not yours to dismiss, Thomas. You made your decision three days ago and I have paid my debt. My only wish is that Samuel Andersen would rise out of his grave and exchange places with you."

"What boldness, lawyer. I didn't think you had it in you." Thomas put the cash in his wallet and folded the bank draft.

"I never dreamed I would have to deal with a man of your evil nature. I have come to realize we are all capable of changing our spots when we are backed into a corner."

"How would you like a job with the Thomas B. Rich Corporation? Starting today. The job pays $20,000 a year with a signing bonus of three thousand and sixty-five dollars if you decide this minute. Well, I am waiting!"

"First you humiliate me and now you want me to work for you? I don't understand."

"I told you before, it is not for you to understand." Thomas unfolded the bank draft and held it in the air between his right thumb and forefinger. "Going once, twice—"

Jamison walked toward him quickly grabbing for the draft. Thomas pulled it back.

"You take this draft and I sign it over to you now. Your debt to me will also be erased. But understand, lawyer, you will work for me. You will do as I say regardless of what you think or feel or do or do not understand, always. Or I swear over the grave of your previous employer, you will regret the day you were born." Thomas held the draft higher.

Jamison was in no position to bargain. He knew he would not be able to make the first payment on his new note and pay back the union boss. His hatred of the man standing before him was so strong, but he was risking his life in the hands of a union mobster for the satisfaction of spitting on the feet of Thomas Rich. Edgar Jamison had no other choice.

"What do I have to do?"

"Drop all of your other clients by Friday and report to my office Monday morning, 7:00 a.m. sharp. My offices are currently in the Wilshire house. Do you understand the terms completely?" Thomas lowered the draft. Edgar Jamison had stopped grabbing for it.

"Yes, Thomas, and I accept the terms."

"Don't ever call me Thomas again. It will be Mr. Rich or sir. And one more thing." He handed the bank draft to Edgar. "Draw up a document transferring your loan from the union boss into my name and name the union man in the document. Bring it with you Monday."

"He'll kill me if I—"

"Then you do not accept the terms of our agreement, Edgar? I thought you said you understood completely. I'll have the bank draft." Thomas reached toward Jamison.

"Yes, sir, I mean no, sir. There is no question as to our agreement. I will have the necessary paperwork ready first thing Monday morning. Forgive me, Mr. Rich. I will not make that mistake again."

"Whoever the asshole is that loaned his membership funds to you will not harm you, Jamison. Wear your best suit Monday. You will be expected to maintain the image of my new company. In fact, I suggest you take the bank draft and buy yourself some new clothes. You will be making enough money to look the part of a corporate attorney and I demand it." Jamison nodded and walked through the cemetery back to his old Chevrolet coupe. Thomas Rich smiled his victory smile.

He smiled in the hot tub also and wondered if he had gotten soft with age. Thinking back on the days when he was young and valiant both giving him virility and strength. He remembered the first official meeting of the new Thomas B. Rich Corporation.

Edgar Jamison was led into the library by a new butler, promptly at 7:00 a.m. Monday. "Jamison, you know Larry Dawkins, I believe. Mr. Dawkins is vice president in charge of acquisitions. You and he will be working very close together. By the way, do you have my document?" Jamison handed Thomas an envelope.

"Thank you for being prompt. You will address Larry as

Mr. Dawkins or sir, publicly and privately. I want anyone in observation of our corporate executives to respect our professionalism and notice the fact that we are better than they are." Thomas opened a file folder and placed it on the desk in front of him.

"Jamison, I want you to go to City Hall this morning. Be there when they open. I want copies of all available records regarding the Petroleum Club in downtown Los Angeles. If the information is not available, then ask around town. Go wherever necessary and find out all you can. I want to know what is on the top floor of the club and if it is available for lease. Larry, go through all of the files regarding land holdings and make sure the necessary paperwork is complete so it can be transferred into the new corporation. This afternoon you and Edgar can go over it to make sure there will be no legal problems. Then research all outstanding loans, and debts to see where we can cut costs and increase income. Any questions?" Both men shook their heads.

"Our next meeting will be at 2:00 p.m. this afternoon." With that Thomas looked down at folder full of information. Without looking up he said, "What are you waiting for? Let's get to work."

The memory of his energy and authority at such a young age produced an instant erection for Thomas. He wished Crystal were there already. He closed his eyes again and was transported back to his first day in business.

At two o'clock in the afternoon, the butler placed fresh lemonade and finger sandwiches on the conference table in front of Thomas's desk. Jamison spoke first.

"The Petroleum Club is owned by the major shareholders in Standard Oil Company of California; i.e. Rockefeller, Exxon; i.e. Rockefeller, Atlantic Refining; i.e. Rockefeller and Socony-Vacuum; i.e. Rockefeller. Basically, the Rockefellers own the club. Membership is by invitation only and it is not passed on to heirs. Last but not least—"

Thomas broke in. "There is hard booze served and there is no one under 21 allowed in the building—yes, I know. That is the reason Samuel always gave when I asked repeatedly to visit the club with him. Go on, Edgar."

"The top floor has twelve private rooms, leased by members wishing to have complete privacy. There are no women allowed in the Petroleum Club; however, a rear entrance and staircase is used to spirit young women to the private quarters. It is a practice that has been maintained since the building was completed in 1920. The private rooms take up one half of the upper floor. The rest of the space is being used as offices, some to run the business of the club; others are used by members upon their request for business purposes. Lastly there is approximately one thousand square feet of storage. That is all I could find out so far."

"Larry, how many of the companies Edgar mentioned have leases with the Andersen Corporation?"

"All of them in one form or another."

"How long has it been since those lease rates have been increased?"

"There has been no increase since the leases were entered into. Most of the leases are coming up for renewal in the next two years. Several are up in a few months. The only one that is currently under re-negotiation is Standard Oil's; it's the oldest lease of the lot."

"Get me all the information and current standing regarding the negotiations as soon as possible, I—"

"Is now too soon? It's all right here in this folder." Larry reached across the desk, handing Thomas a folder five inches thick.

"I knew I had chosen the right man for vice president." Thomas gave a rare grin.

Thomas opened his eyes again. The steam from the hot tub meeting the cool sea air made it look like he was in his own personal fog. He continued to daydream but this time with his eyes wide open. He looked past the steam as it drifted over the balcony. He was young again, taking charge and running roughshod over the old-timers at the Petroleum Club. His memory still sharp, it was as if it was only yesterday.

Within a month, the Thomas B. Rich Corporation moved into what had previously been the storage area on the top floor of the Petroleum Club of Los Angeles. Before the year was out, he had convinced all of the male patrons with families and private suites at the club they were better off leasing their space to Thomas rather than face a scandal. By 1954, there were seven major oil companies controlling 90 percent of the world's oil supply. Of those seven, all had major interests in not only oil drilling, piping and refining in the Los Angeles basin, but they were in dire need of port access as well. In order to do business in Los Angeles in either oil or shipping, a person or his company had to go through a Thomas B. Rich Corporation affiliate. Nothing came in or went out of the City of Angels without adding to the bank account of the richest man in California. By his 30th birthday, Thomas B. Rich was a half billionaire and known as the "Chairman of the Board."

Now, as the eve of the opening of the Thomas B. Rich Museum of Modern Art approached, Thomas knew he was the Rockefeller of the New Age. Besides being the wealthiest man in the United States of America, he was the most powerful. He recalled how he single-handedly broke the back of the trade unions in the 1960s using blackmail and intimidation.

He also remembered how Edgar Jamison had taken his own life by placing a .38 caliber Smith and Wesson to his right temple and pulled the trigger. The note had read, 'I have committed unspeakable acts for my employer and can no longer live with myself.'

Thomas thought out loud, "That weak son of a bitch. He was too much like Samuel when it came to being gallant in the face of true challenge." Thomas stepped from the hot tub and went to the shower in the master bedroom. Shortly thereafter,

Crystal joined him. His day was almost complete.

Across town, Lawrence W. Dawkins, President of Rich Enterprises, was holding Jane Turner in his arms.

"Jane, sweetheart, don't cry anymore. I know what Thomas did was cruel. It's over now. You are your own person. You have a fantastic career and you have me."

Jane wiped her tears again and stood back from Larry. "I know, Larry. You saved my life from that evil man. I don't know how I ever worked for him. I loved him. I wanted to have his child. He forced me to have an abortion and then kicked me back into the streets. If you hadn't come after me and loved me, I don't know where I would be today. I love you. It's just that his ugliness today brought it all back again. I'm sorry."

"No need to apologize, Janie. It's all in the past. I will always take care of you, you know that." Larry stroked her hair and kissed her cheek.

"Yes, I know, Larry. You owe everything to Thomas Rich and I owe everything to you. What do you think would happen if Thomas ever found out about us? I know you always say how I shouldn't worry, but you and I both know how ruthless he can be."

"Jane, our secret is safe. Thomas would be angry but he could never run the business without me. Besides, how could he ever find out? I know his every move and where he is at all times. Right now he's pressing Crystal's back into the tile at the beach house. They'll be having dinner at 'GRANITA' and spend the night at the beach house. In less than six weeks you and I will be in the Greek Islands on one of the most unbelievable sailboats ever built. And we will have it all to ourselves. Cheer up, little one, all is not lost." Larry spoke bravely as always. But deep in his heart he knew how evil Thomas could be. Thinking back to the mid-sixties and seventies when he and Thomas had broken the rail workers union sending their labor force into other unions such as the pipe fitters, steelworkers and electricians.

As those unions gained strength in the oil fields, Thomas, once again with the help of Larry Dawkins, brought in cheap nonunion labor from the South, banishing the union labor from the oil companies and sending those union men in search of other means to feed their families and attempt to maintain a higher standard of living.

Larry knew too well how deep the hate in Thomas B. Rich could run. He would do everything in his power to keep his and Jane's relationship a secret. She was a success in her own right and Thomas was forced to deal with her in a professional setting.

But Larry also knew Thomas's policy regarding his castaways. Once he tired of or felt betrayed by one of his 'Girls on Call,' as he liked to refer to them, they might as well be dead. And Jane Turner was anything but dead.

Chapter 6
The Healer

BILL LARKIN ARRIVED AT the studio around 9:30 p.m. The security guard tipped his hat and opened the gate allowing him entry into the lot. Bill went directly to his office and closed the door behind him. He was looking for a log of the day's top news stories. The stack was usually thick with ideas for follow-up stories, as well as hot ones the network needed to air as soon as they could get confirmation of the story's authenticity. Halfway through the pile he saw the daily. He read the report.

Number 1; Shootout at local market, 2; lost girl found dead, 3; sink hole opens up at site for new underground transportation system (again), 4; Girl survives fatal auto crash on I-5…

"That's the one. Let's see, where is the follow-up," Bill spoke to himself out loud as he turned the pagers.

"Here it is. I-5 accident. Call in witness, unidentified, left a phone number, call in witness No. 2, paramedic, call in witness No. 3, emergency room nurse Mrs. O'Neal. Great, everyone wants their fifteen seconds of fame. She didn't know who I was. Apparently neither did anyone from the station. They must have been waiting for the news conference like all the rest. Ah, here is what I was looking for, aerial footage from Air Five…accident scene I-5, 3:55 p.m."

Bill took the list and file number to the film room. After a few minutes he found the video marked 1-12-96, 3:55 p.m. I-5 aerial. He took the cassette back to his office and loaded it into the VCR on his viewing platform. He ran the tape. The emergency services crew were on the scene. He could make out the paramedics working on his daughter. He pushed the rewind button. He was looking for Susan and spotted her talking to a uniformed officer. Must have been Ken Taylor. He saw Susan breaking away going over to Adrian, pushing others out of the way.

"These shots are unbelievably clear," Bill said to himself. He saw Susan pick up Adrian and start rocking her. The tech, and CHP officers along with some bystanders are watching over Susan and Adrian. A man approaches from the side. Bill rewinds again. A man in a white T-shirt and jeans. "Where did you come from, stranger?" Again he rewinds the tape but in slow motion. Man in T-shirt walking backwards, slower, slower. Picture slows down as Bill pushes the speed button on the remote control in his hand.

The picture starts to distort somewhat. He speeds it up one quarter. The man in the T-shirt steps out of the picture as the helicopter turns back toward the accident. Bill rewinds back to the last overview shot of the accident scene. A white pickup truck is parking next to the center divider about where the man in the T-shirt had walked from. Bill fast forwards the tape. The man in the white T-shirt is kneeling next to Susan and Adrian. Adrian reaches out to Susan and puts her arms around her neck. The man in the white T-shirt stands and walks around the wreck.

The camera pans again. The man gets into the white Ford pickup truck with material racks on it. There are tools and equipment in the bed of the truck, the camera is still panning during its turn back toward the accident, the stranger starts driving away.

"The license plate, zoom in on the license plate," Bill talks to himself out loud. He slows the video to one-eighth speed and blows it up with his state-of-the-art viewing equipment. "The license number." Again Bill rewinds the tape to the point of the truck pulling away, zooming in on the license number. "Freeze, 7H11854, California plate." Bill tracks up to half speed and rewinds. Susan wraps her arms around Adrian stroking her hair. Bill starts crying and bows his head as the video continues.

Bill Larkin was not sure what he had seen on the video. He ran the tape back to when the stranger enters the picture and stopped the tape. As he pushed play, he slowed it down and watched the tape through until it moved away from the scene. He paid close attention to the audio portion of the tape to see if the traffic reporter noticed anything unusual. There was no mention of a miraculous occurrence in the report.

From that distance and in a moving helicopter it would be impossible to realize the drama unfolding down on the pavement. Bill ran it back to the frame where the license plate on the truck was visible.

"7H11854." He spoke the number as he wrote it. Bill ran the tape back to the beginning and returned it to the carrying case. Unable to decide whether or not he should put the tape back in the storage room, he decided to place the case with the tape under a pile of empty video shipping boxes.

"Maybe this will give me the time I need to find out what really happened on the freeway today," Bill said to himself. He went back to his office and picked up a small pocket recorder. Bill checked his pocket for the paper with the license plate number written on it as he added two empty audiotapes just in case. He turned off the light in his office and headed for the main building of the Los Angeles Police Department downtown.

During the drive, Bill reflected over and over what he had seen or not seen in the videotape. Again he spoke to himself. "Stranger, I hope what I am about to do does not destroy you, but I have to know what happened to my wife and daughter today."

Bill entered the main lobby of the first precinct around 10:45 p.m. He recognized the officer at the counter and the officer recognized Bill.

"Well, look who we have here. Mr. Larkin, KBLA news. What are you doing out at this hour?" The officer sounded impressed and honorary. "I thought the boss stayed in nights and had those pesky reporters running around in the dark."

Bill Larkin smiled and extended his hand. "Sergeant Mitchell, how are you this evening?" Bill served his famous smile of professional courtesy not knowing if the sergeant was truly friend or foe.

"I'm doing good, Mr. Larkin, very good indeed." Mitchell gave him a hearty handshake back. "What can I do for you?"

"Actually, Sergeant, I need a small favor. I was hoping you could discreetly help me." Bill placed his hands in the pockets of his sport coat.

The sergeant placed the paperwork in his hand aside. Squinting at Bill as he spoke. "You know that piece you did on Officer Wilkenson was really appreciated around the cop corps. It had been a long time since an officer in this city was killed in the line of duty and Wilkerson was a good cop. Your report and the reward information you gave out was a great help to the department and his family." Sergeant Mitchell paused and took a deep breath.

"You even showed up to his funeral. That went a long way around here I'll have you know, Mr. Larkin, a long way. What favor can I do for you?"

Bill handed him the piece of paper with the license number printed on it. "Could you find an address to go with this license plate number? I would be very grateful if we could keep this between the two of us, if you know what I mean."

"Sure, I know what you mean. I know Lieutenant Conners is an old friend of yours from school and he pulls up numbers for you now and again. I have no problem with that. You know it is illegal for us to give a home address out to regular citizens. You're not planning anything against this guy, are you?"

"No, of course not." Bill was almost sorry he hadn't waited for Jerry Conners. However, Jerry worked days and this couldn't wait.

"If you would rather wait until I speak with Lieutenant Conners in the morning, I'll wait."

"No, no that isn't what I meant at all. I just wanted it understood that if this ever comes back to me, I don't know a thing. Is it a California plate?"

"Yes, and it is current." Bill felt better. He did not want to be in the station house long enough to be seen by members of his or any other news staff.

"Here it is, Mr. Larkin." The sergeant cocked his head back so he could read through his corrective lenses. "Looks like a Mr. Paul Iscariot, 1196 Palm Court, Los Angeles, California. Phone number, do you want his phone number?" he said without looking up.

"Yes, please, any information you have will be helpful."

"OK, I'll write it down. As long as I'm in here, I'll run his rap sheet to see what kind of man you're dealing with." The sergeant hen pecked out several series of numbers and letters on the computer keyboard.

"Well, it looks like he has a clean record. Whoa, wait a minute here. I've never seen one of these before!"

Bill leaned over the counter. "What is it?"

"This Iscariot guy has the Presidential Seal on his sheet." Sergeant Mitchell sounded impressed. "As in the President of the United States of America seal."

"What does that mean?" Bill asked.

"Well, it means anything short of murder this guy walks. No questions asked." Mitchell whistled. "I'm serious about this not coming back to me, Mr. Larkin. We got a deal?"

"Don't worry, Sergeant. I don't want it coming back on me

either." Bill reached out and took the computer sheet from Mitchell's hand.

Mitchell grabbed after it. "Hey, I can't—"

Bill cut him off. "Thank you, Sergeant Mitchell, you have been a great help. I'll show myself out." Bill was halfway across the lobby and out the door before Sergeant Mitchell could respond.

Bill strode two steps at a time up the stairs of the parking structure to his car. His map book was in the trunk and he retrieved it before he sat in the driver's seat.

"Let's see, 1196 Palm Court." He ran his finger down the 'P' page. "Palm Court. Palm Court. Here it is." He turned to the referenced page and crossed E-5. "So our stranger lives right in the middle of the barrio."

It was after one o'clock in the morning on Saturday by the time Bill Larkin drove down Palm Court and parked in front of number 1196. He turned off the engine and stared at the house. It was a plain white, wood sided home with a composition roof. There was a four foot high chainlink fence surrounding the front yard and narrow driveway. The lawn was trimmed and well cared for as were the numerous rosebushes down the drive and around the front of the house. The homes around number 1196 were also very neat and well maintained. The people living in the neighborhood took obvious pride in their homes. Bill thought to himself how television and feature films color a person's perception regarding other nationalities. Even if American born, a person with a Spanish surname conjures up fears of gangs, drugs and violence.

"Has the media poisoned us to the point that we generalize everyone by the way they look or the color of their skin?" Bill wondered out loud. His thoughts continued.

During the last riot, after the King verdict, the neighborhoods were out of control. Even with the cameras rolling, thieves, local people—hell, even some from this neighborhood were looting and vandalizing community stores.

They destroyed the shops and buildings they need every day to survive. I don't get it. Are we so frustrated and angry that one spark can ignite death and destruction in a country as great as America? I realize a handful of bad seeds can make an entire society look pathetic. The reality of it is, these people are also my neighbors. Who steps up and takes responsibility?

"Our politicians are so corrupt we can't depend on their integrity to lead or protect us. Who do we turn to for help? The jails are overcrowded, the police are overburdened and we are all overtaxed. Where does it all end?" Bill felt drained and suddenly realized he was talking to himself.

He looked at his watch, it was 2:15 a.m. Bill decided against a call to Susan. The white pickup truck was sitting inside the fence up near the garage. Bill decided to wait and knock on the stranger's door in the morning. He reached down next to the car door and felt for the lever on the side of the seat. One light touch and the seat laid out almost flat. Using the electronic controls, Bill moved the seat back as far as he could away from the dash to stretch out his legs. He checked the door locks and cracked the driver's side window. He was thinking of how good some of Jack Swanson's spaghetti would taste right now when he fell asleep.

A loud noise woke Bill. Another pickup had parked across the street directly in front 1196. The apparent owner was a large Hispanic-looking gentleman in bib overalls and a T-shirt. He had dropped the tailgate of the truck so he could tie his work boots from a better angle than bending all the way over. Bill looked past the man toward the front porch of the house matching the address he received at the police station.

"Hey, Manny, are you ready to go or do you need some help tying your boots?"

A handsome man, with light skin and brownish hair, wearing jeans and a gray sweatshirt, stood on the porch with a glass of what looked like orange juice.

The large man yelled back, "Pablito. What do you expect

when you call these early morning mercy missions? I could barely get out of bed after all of the work I had to do this week." Manny grunted trying to get his right foot up as high as the tailgate.

"Do you want some breakfast or are you still on the 'diet'?" Pablito laughed and motioned Manny to come into the house.

"No, amigo, I don't want no breakfast. I want to go to the donut store for one of those strawberry pastries. You said if I was on time, you would buy. Well, I'm on time!" Manny slammed the tailgate and walked toward the house shaking out his pant legs.

Bill thought, *So, our stranger Pablito, Paul, is a construction worker. How could Susan think in her educated mind that a man off the street returned our daughter to the living? Between the reports of all the technicians present and my own wife...* Bill scratched his head. He also rubbed the sleep out of his eyes, rearranged the driver's seat and put on his dark glasses. He had decided to introduce himself to the stranger, Mr. Paul Iscariot, and ask to speak to him alone.

As he opened the door to leave the car, he checked his watch. It was 7:15 a.m. Jack would be up waiting for his pancakes to brown and if Susan was on her usual schedule, she would be sitting in the kitchen on her second cup of tea. It never ceased to amaze Bill how Susan could get up at the crack of dawn with a smile, a tune on her lips and be readying the day, no matter how late she went to bed. He figured he had better call on his cell phone before he went to meet 'Pablito.' The phone rang once.

"Hello, Jack?"

"Billy boy, where the hell are you? I've been up most the night waiting to hear from you. Are you OK?" Jack sounded worried but with his usual exuberance it was always hard to tell panic from parenthood.

"Yes, I'm fine. Is Susan with you?"

"Yes, yes, she's right here. Did you find the stranger?" Jack wanted the news so he could give it to Susan. "Wait a minute, Billy boy, Susan wants to talk to you." Jack handed the phone to Susan.

"Bill, are you all right?" Susan showed concern in her voice.

"Yes, sweetheart, I am fine. I just fell asleep in the car and lost track of time. How are the children and how are you?"

"We're all fine. The boys are eating pancakes and Adrian is still asleep. She slept with me last night and never moved a muscle. I am just amazed, Bill. Did you find the stranger yet?"

"Yes, in fact, I slept in front of his house last night and I am just going to talk to him now."

"Bill, what's his name?" Susan started to cry.

"I want to make sure first, Susan. You take it easy today and after I find out more, I promise I will call you. Trust me, sweetheart. OK?"

"I trust you, Bill. Do me a favor? Come here with the news, I don't want to hear it over the phone. Would you do that for me?" Susan was steady and serious.

"Yes, of course I will, Susan. Whatever you want." Bill looked out the window toward the house on Palm Court.

Susan continued. "I want to see your face when you tell me what you found out. I want to know if what I have been feeling is correct, OK? One more thing, tell him thank you."

"Suz, I have to go. He's coming out of the house. I promise, as soon as I find out what happened, I will come to you and tell you in person. I love you."

Bill was hanging up the phone and trying to get out of the car at the same moment Susan said, "I love you too."

Before Bill could untangle from the seat belt and lock the car, Paul, Manny, and a third person were backed out of the driveway in Paul's truck and headed down the street. Bill quickly unlocked the Lexus, started the engine, and made a U-turn. He just missed the truck at the corner turning onto Main Street and heading toward the 105 Freeway. Bill stopped briefly at the red light and sped around the corner before he lost sight of 7H11854. Before the freeway entrance Bill saw the truck's brake lights flash on. They were turning into a small strip shopping center prior to the stoplight. Bill followed. Paul parked his truck in front of a Donut Inn. He, Manny and a boy around 17 got out of the pickup and walked into the donut shop. Bill backed his car into a space facing the shop. When he saw Paul and his crew sit down at a table, he decided to go in and get a large coffee and something to eat. He had a feeling it might be a long day before he would have a chance to meet Paul Iscariot alone. He entered the shop and approached the counter.

"May I help you, sir?" asked the young girl.

"Yes, please. May I have a large black coffee and a cinnamon roll to go?" Bill looked nonchalantly around the store trying to get a closer look at the stranger. He was thinking of how it felt knowing the stranger's name, address, and phone number, when he caught Paul's eye from where he was sitting in the booth. Paul smiled and resumed his conversation with the boy.

"Here you are, sir. Will there be anything else?" the girl asked.

"Do you have Equal and a napkin?" Bill realized he also had to use a men's room. He glanced toward the booth where Paul was sitting to see if they were getting ready to leave. With doughnuts and coffee still plentiful at their table, he turned and asked, "Is there a restroom?"

"Yes, sir. The Equal and napkins are on the end of the counter and the restroom is outside around the back. You need a key." She smiled and handed Bill the key with a huge wooden key chained to it. The girl saw Bill's reaction to the wood key and said, "That's so you don't forget to bring it back! If you want I will keep your coffee and roll until you return."

"You're an angel." Bill started toward the door. "Oh, how much do I owe you?" He turned as he reached for his wallet.

"Two eighty-five," she smiled.

Bill had five dollars in his hand and put it on the counter in front of her. "Keep the change, young lady, and thanks for the service." Bill headed for the door. He did not want to lose Paul after spending the night in his car. The girl was all smiles. Bill hurried as he returned with the key. He noticed that Paul and the young man had already gone out to the truck. Manny lagged behind getting one for the road. Bill put the key on the counter picking up his coffee and roll.

The girl behind the counter said, "Thank you very much, mister. Please come again."

He passed by the napkins and sweetener walking quickly to his car. In the parking lot he felt the eyes of the stranger watching him. Setting the coffee on the roof of the car to free up a hand for his keys, he noticed, in the reflection on his windshield, the stranger was walking toward him. He continued to gather his coffee and roll, bracing himself with his leg, holding the keys in his mouth, trying to ready himself to leave instantly. He looked toward the truck, the stranger was gone.

Manny and the boy sat with the driver's side door open laughing about something. Bill closed his door, put the key in the ignition and set the coffee in a cup holder located in the ashtray. He turned on the ignition and started the car. He looked in the side view mirror and saw the stranger walking close to the driver's side of the car. As the stranger approached, Bill lowered the window.

"Good morning." The stranger's voice was solemn yet friendly.

"Yes, good morning to you." Bill was a little off-guard.

"May I help you with something?" the stranger asked.

"What do you mean?" Bill turned his head looking up at Paul.

"I noticed you parked in front of my house and then here at the doughnut store. I thought maybe there was something you wanted." The stranger bent down so Bill could look at him eye to eye.

"Truthfully I would like to talk to you." Bill turned off the ignition and sat back in the seat. "My daughter was the little girl in the accident yesterday."

"How is she?" the stranger asked.

"She is fine. There is nothing wrong with her. That's why I am here. My wife says you performed a miracle. Several professional eyewitnesses say the same thing."

"What do you believe?" The stranger stood and opened the car door as Bill stepped out.

"Frankly, I don't know what to believe. I wanted to ask you some questions before I jump to any conclusions." Bill reached out his hand. "I'm Bill Larkin."

"Bill, I'm Paul Iscariot," he said, shaking Bill's hand. "But then you must already know my name if you have my address. By the way, how did you find me so quickly?"

Bill explained about the videotape and a contact at the police department. "I'm sorry. I should have called you and asked to speak to you. I am struggling with the fact that I am a father and a newsman in this situation. I'm sure you can understand."

"It explains the answer to my next question."

Bill looked puzzled and asked, "What was your next question?"

"Why no news crew?" Paul smiled. "It has been the great underground quest by news people for centuries to uncover my family's history. The press trying to get the Iscariot story."

Bill put on his newsman's face. "What is the story, Paul Iscariot?" Bill turned on the pocket recorder in his left coat pocket.

"Are you going to ask me if you can record this conversation?" Paul looked amused.

"Are you also a mind reader?" Bill asked as he pulled the recorder out in the open.

"No. I do have excellent hearing however and the click of a record button was not hidden in your coat pocket," Paul smiled.

"Will you tell me what happened yesterday, Mr. Iscariot? I won't divulge any of our conversation until I am sure it is the truth and truth is what the news is all about."

"No offense, Mr. Larkin, because your news may be different. From my observation, the news is anything but the truth. It's the news. No matter whatever, or whenever. Correct me if I'm wrong."

Bill looked away and drew a deep breath as he took the recorder from his pocket and turned it off. "I can't say you are wrong. I know what you mean. People do have a right to know what is going on in the world."

Paul folded his arms and spoke directly into Bill's face. "Do you think the people have to know everything? Sometimes, things have a way of correcting themselves if people stay uninformed."

"That is true, yet some things of which they are least informed about are the things they need to know the most. Don't you agree?" Bill stared back directly into Paul's eyes.

Paul relaxed and smiled again. "Well perhaps. But I'm not big on debate. Can I call you Bill?"

"Yes, of course, Mr. Iscariot."

"Please, Bill, call me Paul."

"OK, Paul. Can you tell me what happened yesterday with my daughter?"

"It's not that simple." Paul grew serious again.

"I didn't think it would be. Why don't you start at the beginning." Bill set the recorder in the roof of his car and switched it on.

Paul smiled broadly. "Wait a minute, father/newsman. The beginning goes back to the year—well, it goes back a ways. I have a promise to keep with Manny and my son. We are going to the Rescue Mission and put in some new shelves for a friend of mine. You should probably go home and get some rest. Spend some time with your family. What are you doing later this evening?"

"No plans at the moment. Why do you ask?" Bill switched off the recorder.

"Every other Saturday I go down to the Junkyard and meet with the sick children and others. I am going tonight. Would you like to come along? I'll tell you as much as I can in the few hours we spend together." Paul reached into his pocket for his keys.

"I'll come. Where do we meet and when?" Bill was sensing a story to beat all stories. A Pulitzer Prize perhaps.

"Say my house 6:00 p.m.?" Paul reached out to shake his hand.

"Six sharp, I will see you then. Can I bring my recorder?"

"I'll let you decide, Bill. See you at six." Paul turned and walked toward his truck. He stopped and turned back, half shouting at Bill, "Bill, what is your wife's name?"

"It's Susan. Why do you ask?"

"Tell Susan, her prayer was answered. I'll see you tonight." Bill stood there and watched the man that may have very well saved his daughter's life drive away.

Chapter 7
Paul Iscariot LXXV

BILL ARRIVED AT HIS in-laws' house around noon. He had gone back to the studio to find the best pocket recorder available with a remote microphone. It would give him the best sound quality and the most tape capacity. There was a message on his voice mail.

"Bill, Stan. What do you think of the I-5 story? I put two and two together. The guard said you were in last night and I thought you were going south for a soccer tournament. I saw on the news where a girl named Larkin was saved by a miracle and no one knows anything about it. I figured the only way something like this can be kept from the media, is if the media is keeping it from the media. Call me." Stan was Bill Larkin's boss. He ran advertising and sales. News was big sales. Bill decided he would call him after his meeting with Paul Iscariot.

When Bill arrived at the Swanson home, he noticed the children and their grandfather in the back corner of the lot harvesting some kind of fruit. Jack loved fresh fruit and vegetables. His garden was the pride and joy of both he and Elaine. The front door was unlocked, as usual. He let himself in quietly in case Susan was napping. Bill looked in the bedroom and Susan was not there. He checked the living room, kitchen and the garage. Elaine's car was gone. Maybe the two of them had gone to the grocery store. Bill walked to the back of the house where the master bedroom faced the rear yard and saw his wife sitting in a rocking chair.

He spoke softly. "Susan, are you awake?" Susan continued to rock. "Suz, honey, are you OK?" Susan turned to look at Bill and her cheeks were wet from tears. "Hey, I thought you would be all cried out by now. What's the matter?" Bill took Susan in his arms.

She looked over his shoulder at the children running in the yard. "Adrian's life was a gift given back to her mother. She was gone, Bill, I know it as sure as I am standing here. I can't take my eyes off her. Dad says that God works in mysterious ways and it is not for us to question. I'm not questioning. I am so grateful I don't know what to do."

"Do what you have always done. Be the best mother and wife any family could ever have." Bill kissed her tears and moved a strand of curled hair from the side of her right cheek. "I'm grateful too, sweetheart. I am grateful all of you are alive and here right this minute."

"Did you talk to the stranger?" Susan stopped crying.

"Yes, I did." Bill helped her sit down in the rocker and pulled a chair over to sit in front of her.

"What is his name?" Susan focused now on Bill's eyes and facial expressions.

"His name is Paul Iscariot."

"You mean like Judas Iscariot, the man that betrayed Jesus?"

"I don't know. Was his name Iscariot?"

"Yes. Go on." Susan was holding both of Bill's hands and leaning toward him.

"He lives in Los Angeles, in the barrio, he is in construction and he has a son named—I didn't get his son's name. Tonight I will be sure and ask him."

"Tonight, what is happening tonight? Is he coming over?" Susan was excited.

"No. I am going to meet him at his house. He is taking me someplace where he works, I guess." Bill realized he hadn't gotten much information.

"Bill Larkin, you never guess. You always know. You are the newsman that always knows. Tell me what he said, please!"

Bill sat back in the chair. "He asked how you and Adrian were and the boys and then we talked."

"Did he say anything about yesterday?" Susan couldn't believe he had so little information to tell her.

"No, he didn't. We kind of talked about people in general and the media." Bill seemed dumbfounded.

"Well, this is a first. The famous newsman with no story." Susan showed her disappointment.

"Suz, I'm sorry. I was going to record our conversation but he heard me switch the recorder on. I took it out of my pocket and switched it off. He was on his way to the Mission District to put in some shelves for a friend. Actually he was going to the Rescue Mission."

"Is that all he said? He didn't tell you how he gave Adrian back to us or anything?"

"There was one thing. As he turned to go, he called back and asked me your name. Then he said, 'Tell Susan her prayer was answered.'"

Susan sat back in the chair and started crying.

Jack came bursting into the room. "Susan, honey, I got a big red apple here with your name on it. Hey, Billy, you're back. What did you find out? Did the guy really heal our little Adrian?"

"I don't know, Jack. I didn't ask him."

"You didn't ask him? Wouldn't he talk to you, Billy? Let's go back and see him together."

Bill stood up and took Adrian in his arms. "I am going to see him later this evening. I'll have plenty of time to ask him then."

"Tonight?" Jack grew even more excited. "What's

happening tonight? Is he coming over?"

Adrian took her daddy's face in both hands and made herself nose to nose with him. "Is that true, Daddy? Is he coming here tonight?"

"No, baby girl, he is not coming here. I am going to work with him tonight."

"Great, Billy, we can both work with him tonight. I have a few questions of my own to ask him." Jack was rubbing his hands together. "I also want him to know if there is anything I can ever do for him that all of my resources are available. What time do we leave?"

Bill moved close to his father-in-law. "Jack, please don't take offence to this but I have to see him alone. I don't know what is going to happen when we get together and I want him to feel free to talk openly with me. Another person along might make him less talkative. Do you know what I mean?"

"Yes, I know what you mean. I just want this miracle man to know how much it means to me. You know, what he did for my Adrian."

"I will make you the same promise I made Susan. In fact, I will make the three of you the same promise. I will tell Mr. Iscariot we are all grateful and we will be available to assist him in any contribution or time we can afford. First I want to understand what happened. So far our conclusions are purely speculative and I can't accept speculation. I will find out everything I can tonight and share it with you all tomorrow. Fair enough? Susan, Jack, baby girl?"

"The guy's name is Iscariot? Like the fellow in the Bible? You know Judas." Jack's mind and enthusiasm was working faster than his mouth.

"Let's look it up, Jack. Do you have a Bible?" Bill was trying to move on to another outlet for Jack to keep him involved without participating directly with the stranger.

"I have one, Bill. I was reading the New Testament when you came in." Susan handed it to her father. "I was reading about Jesus and his work among the poor and sick. Bill, do you suppose Mr. Iscariot is really…"

"Susan, we can't suppose anything. I want all of us to take this one step at a time. I will find out tonight what happened yesterday. Jack, before you get too deep into the Bible, do you suppose you could heat up some of your leftover meatballs and make me a sandwich? I spent the night in the car and all I have had since breakfast yesterday is a large coffee and part of a cinnamon roll."

"You bet, son. I'm sorry for jumping ahead of you I just…" Jack took Bill by the hand and, with a tear on each cheek, embraced him.

"I know, Jack. The only thing I am sure of right this minute is Susan, Adrian and the boys are here and well. We couldn't go through this without you and Elaine. You are the best parents and grandparents anyone could have. I mean it." Bill embraced Jack and patted him on the back.

Jack was choked up but only for a minute. "I will make you a great meatball sandwich. How about a fresh green salad to go with it?"

"That sounds terrific, Chef Swanson. I'll be right behind you. First I want to talk to Susan." Bill handed Adrian to Jack.

"Come on, little girl chef, help Grandpa with your dad's lunch." Jack and Adrian went to the kitchen.

"I meant what I said about your dad, Susan. He is one in a million. He and Elaine—I really don't know what we would do without them. Over the years I have been fairly impatient with your dad's energetic rush at life. Do you think I can make it up to him?"

"You don't have anything to make up to him, Bill. He thinks you are the best husband a daughter could have. They both love you and so do I." Susan stood and embraced Bill. She put her mouth up to his and began a long, loving kiss.

Bill returned the display of affection. "Where were you last night when I was sitting all alone in that car?" Bill kissed

Susan again. "By the way, did Dr. Lewis make it last night?"

"Yes, he did." Susan continued her kiss.

"What did he say? Is everything all right?" Bill tried to stand back to look at Susan's face. She tightened her grip around his neck.

Between a breath and more of the kiss, she replied, "Yes, we are all fine."

"Did he take your blood pressure and check the kids?" Bill asked, still trying to push back.

"Our blood pressure was normal. Right now, however, mine is starting to rise. Too bad I can't say the same for you." Susan kissed him more passionately as she hugged Bill even tighter.

"Maybe we should go into our room and continue this conversation. I don't want your dad or Adrian walking in on us."

"What are you expecting, Mr. Larkin? You spent the entire night out and come dragging in here after noon, with no information and you expect me to be a pushover?" Susan released Bill's neck.

"The way things were going I thought…"

"Let me do the thinking right now." Susan took Bill's hand and started for the hall.

"Dad, will you keep and eye on the kids for me for a while? Billy and I are going to take a nap."

Jack looked around the corner from the kitchen down the hall. "Sure, but what about Bill's lunch?" Jack was in his apron.

"Just keep it warm for him. He wants room service later."

Jack spoke to himself as the bedroom door shut behind Susan and Bill. "Sounds like he's going to get room service right now. Those two will never grow up."

Elaine came in from the garage as Jack continued to talk to himself. "Come to think of it I'll never grow up." He walked to Elaine and took a grocery bag from her right arm. "Hey, beautiful, want to take a nap?" The more passionately he kissed her the wider her eyes grew.

After Bill and Susan made love, they slept deeper than they ever remembered. Susan woke first. "Bill, Bill, sweetheart, it's 5:00 o'clock. Aren't you supposed to meet Mr. Iscariot at six?"

"Yes, six this evening." Bill stretched and tried to shake the cobwebs from his head. "I feel like I did when we used to pass out for an entire weekend. I didn't have any wine with lunch, did I?" Bill could not remember.

"Not only did you not have any wine, you missed lunch." Susan kissed Bill soft and deep with one more passionate kiss. "There, can you think of a better way to wake up?"

"Susan, I love you. I have been spending a lot of time away the last couple of years. You never complain and always keep me posted as to who's playing where, when and what. After this last couple of days, well maybe…"

"Maybe what? You should look for another job? I like you the way you are. If you were back on the street as a reporter or a sports commentator, I don't think I could stand it. You may not always be home at a decent hour but you are home every night. You don't travel except on the rare occasion for a management seminar or an award banquet and then the folks watch the kids and I get to go with you.

"If you weren't in charge of KBLA news you would go crazy. You are the best and you love it. The children keep me busy and the museum is a pleasant distraction. As a matter of fact, I am becoming quite the curator of fine art. Allison Rich asked me to find a Renoir and I found one in Washington, D.C. It's in the White House."

Bill grinned at her. "And you think you can buy a painting from the President?" Bill swung out of bed and walked to the bathroom. He picked up a razor and started the shower.

"No, I don't think I can buy a painting from the President. Mrs. Rich believes her husband can request, in writing, for me to see the painting and ask if we can hang it in the new gallery for the grand opening."

"Will you invite me along to meet the President?" Bill spoke over the shower.

"It depends." Susan had wrapped her long dark hair in a towel and stepped into the shower with Bill. She took the soap from him and started rubbing his back.

"Depends on what? If I wash your back or not?" Bill reached for the soap but Susan dropped it intentionally.

"No. It depends on how good of a reporter you turn out to be." Susan put her arms around Bill's neck.

"You just said a minute ago that I was the best damn reporter you knew." Bill pulled her body tight to his.

"That was before. This is now." Susan smiled and licked her lips settling her hips against her husband's.

"What's now that wasn't fifteen minutes ago?" Bill smiled back and kissed her.

"If you're late for your appointment and miss the story of the stranger or if you don't ask questions this time or…"

Bill let go of Susan and reached through the shower door for a towel. "I almost forgot. You, my dear, are a career-ending distraction." Bill dried and dressed as Susan turned off the water and stood in front of him naked and dripping wet. "You are also the most beautiful 'old' art curator I have ever seen. I'll call you if I am going to be late. Give the kids a kiss for me will you and tell Jack I'll eat when I get home."

Susan smiled and put on a robe following Bill out of the bedroom. Eric and Bill Junior were sitting on the front porch.

"What are you guys waiting for?" Bill asked.

"Grandpa. He said we were going to hike up to Grandpa Rock. He and Grandma went to take a nap but that was over an hour ago."

Bill looked back at Susan and smiled, "Like father, like daughter." Susan returned his smile. "Where is your sister? I want to say good-bye." Bill hugged both of the boys.

"She's in the garden staring at the flowers."

Bill started around the side of the house to see his daughter.

She was standing in the middle of the rosebushes with her eyes closed and sunning her face in the evening sun.

"Hey, baby girl, Daddy is leaving now. I'll see you in the morning. OK?"

Adrian opened her eyes and looked at her father. "Be careful, Daddy, and give the stranger a big hug for me."

Bill picked her up and held her tightly. "If all goes well tonight, sweetheart, you will get to hug the stranger yourself." Bill kissed her cheek.

"You promise?"

Bill smiled and set her back on the ground. "Yes, I promise."

"I love you, Daddy." Adrian blew him a kiss as he walked back to the front yard.

"I love you too, Adrian." A tear welled up in Bill's left eye. When he returned to the front porch, Jack, Susan and the boys were waiting for him.

Jack had a large paper bag cradled in his left arm and a smaller sack in his right hand. "Billy, I packed you a sandwich and put some apples in a bag for Paul and his family. Be careful and if you need anything call me."

Bill took the bags and thanked Jack. "I am sure the Iscariots will appreciate the apples, Jack. I'll be sure and call if I need anything. Thanks for the meatball sandwich." Bill kissed Susan one more time and turned toward the car.

"That's not a meatball sandwich in there, Billy. I ate that myself. I put a fresh tomato from the garden and some bacon on a piece of lettuce in the bag. There is a piece of cake and an apple in there too."

Bill smiled broadly at his father-in-law. "You did all of this and got in a nap too? I'll tell you, Jack, I can't wait to retire and have as much energy as you have."

Jack turned red momentarily and yelled, "Amen to that, Billy, amen to that."

Once Bill was under way he looked at his watch. It was ten

minutes to six. He opened the file folder on the front seat of his car and looked for Paul Iscariot's phone number. It rang three times.

"Hello." It was a female voice slightly raspy but genuine and with a sweet quality.

"Hello, this is Bill Larkin. Is Paul home?" Bill did not like being late for any appointment.

"Yes, Mr. Larkin, Paul is out front waiting for you. I will tell him you are on the phone."

"No, please. I am only ten or fifteen minutes late. I just wanted to let him know I was on the way. Do you think he will mind?"

"No, Mr. Larkin. My Paul is a patient man. He is looking forward to having you along this evening. I will tell him you called."

Bill was relieved. "Thank you so much. Are you Mrs. Iscariot?" Bill asked.

"Yes, I am. However, I am Paul's mother, not his spouse. Sometimes people call and think they are talking to Paul's wife." Bill detected a slight accent in her words.

"I am looking forward to meeting you, Mrs. Iscariot. Please relay my message to Paul and my apology for being late."

"Do not worry, Mr. Larkin. He was going to make you wait when you got here anyway. I have a fresh apple pie in the oven and he will not leave until he has a piece. Do you like home-baked apple pie, Mr. Larkin?" She had a mother's knowing tone in her voice.

"I love homemade apple pie. Can I bring anything? Say vanilla ice cream or milk?" Bill was trying earnestly to make up for being late.

"No thank you, Mr. Larkin. Just bring your appetite for hot apple pie. We will be waiting."

"I will be there in less than ten minutes." Bill returned the cell phone to its cradle and noticed the bag of Jack's green apples on the floor next to the front seat. It must be his newsman's luck to have pie waiting and fresh apples for the stranger's mother when he arrives. He thought about calling Susan but decided to wait until he saw her. Paul Iscariot was in the front yard with a garden hose watering the roses when Bill parked in front of the house.

"Hello, Bill." Paul waved.

Bill thought, *This family seems just like any other family living the struggle of the American dream. What makes Paul Iscariot such an unknown quantity? There must be a logical explanation for what he did with Adrian.*

"Hello, Paul. I am sorry I'm late. I took your advice and went back to the house to rest. I also spent some time with my family. I was going to eat but the time got away from me and…"

"I am sure my mother has plenty of food left over from dinner. Would you like to have her warm something for you?"

"No thank you. My father-in-law made me a BLT. I ate it on the way. Your mother did mention she had a fresh apple pie coming out of the oven." Bill opened the passenger side door and retrieved the bag of apples. "Jack sent along some of his homegrown apples. I guess I have come to the right house."

"Jack?" Paul opened the gate for Bill.

"Jack Swanson, he is Susan's father. He has a huge lot with fruit trees and vegetables. He just picked these and insisted I bring them along."

Paul smiled his gentle smile and took the sack from Bill. "I am sure my mother will put these to good use. It sounds like you have a very generous family."

"Yes, they are. And they are eternally grateful for what you did yesterday. Which allows me to ask, what did you do yesterday?" Paul spoke softly.

"Why don't we wait until we are on our way before we get in the question and answer period?" Paul sounded as if this was not the first time he had faced an inquiry regarding his special ability. If in fact he had a special ability.

The two men walked through the front door to be greeted by the smell of hot baked apple pie. Paul smacked his lips. "Bill, I love the smell of hot apple pie. Almost as much as I love to eat it." Both men laughed.

Paul was so normal, his surroundings so typical. Bill was starting to feel as if he had the wrong person.

"Bill Larkin, this is my mother, Roxanne Iscariot."

Mrs. Iscariot extended her hand as she wiped it with her apron. "Mr. Larkin, it is a true pleasure having you in our home."

Bill shook her hand. "Thank you, Mrs. Iscariot. Please call me Bill."

"Look, Mother, Susan's father sent you a bag of homegrown apples. Looks like a week, maybe two weeks worth of fresh apple pies." Paul set them down in the sink.

"You eat too much pie as it is. I saw you holding back on dinner to save room for pie. You two go wash up and I will put the pie on the table." Roxanne walked back to the oven.

"Paul, you lead such a normal life. This all seems so regular. House, truck, fence, roses, a mother that cooks pie..." Bill stood there with his arms spread as he summed up the life of Paul Iscariot.

"What did you expect?" Paul smiled as he led Bill toward the bathroom to wash up.

"Expect, I don't know. A parting sea, tablets of rock with the commandments on them. Nothing would have surprised me but this. You're a regular guy." Bill was confounded.

"Actually, I am a regular guy. The difference is I have sure knowledge of things other men only profess to know." Paul took a towel and dried his hands.

"A sure knowledge of what? God?" Bill looked at Paul's reflection in the bathroom mirror. He was looking at his hands as though Bill's question was routine.

"In a way, yes."

Bill turned off the water in the sink and turned to face him.

"You mean you talk to God?" Bill stood there dripping water on the floor from his hands. Paul handed him his towel.

"No not in the way you mean." Reaching out to take the towel back, Paul changes the subject. "Come on, let's get some of that pie while it's hot."

Bill and Paul finished their pie and said good-bye to Paul's mother.

"Why don't you ride in the truck with me, Bill? It will be easier that way and you won't worry about your car."

"Are we going back to the Mission District?" Bill asked sincerely.

"No. We are going down to San Pedro under the Terminal Island Bridge. It's a place known as the 'Junkyard.' It isn't the best place to bring a car as nice as yours. Night brings out the truly needy and usually they take whatever they need. Do you have a coat?" Paul was checking the batteries in two of his four flashlights.

"I have a sweatshirt I use at the gym." Bill retrieved it from his Lexus. "I would like to take my cell phone also if that is all right."

Paul smiled at him. "Sure bring it along. It may come in handy. Does it have an extra battery?" Paul put several bundles in the back of the truck.

"Yes, and it has a full charge. May I bring my recorder as well?"

Bill felt he was pushing it until Paul spoke up. "Yes, by all means. It will definitely come in handy tonight." Paul motioned for Bill to get in the pickup and Bill locked his car.

"Is it OK to leave my car here?" Bill thought he should ask. "Yes."

Paul backed the truck out of the driveway and drove to the Harbor Freeway. Once on the freeway they headed west toward Los Angeles Harbor. Bill fixed the microphone to the collar of his shirt and attached it to the recorder in his shirt pocket.

"Is it all right to record our conversations this evening,

Paul? If it isn't, I won't. I want you to be honest with me. Not that I am questioning your honesty. I just want you to tell me what is comfortable and what isn't." Bill held the palm size recorder and a blank tape in front of him.

"Bill, I will be honest with you tonight and I want you to be honest with me. Most important I want you to be honest with yourself. It is important that the things we discuss or don't discuss be recorded accurately in case you decide what you find out tonight is worth feeding to the public. Agreed?"

"Yes, I heartily agree." Bill put the new ninety-minute tape in the recorder and pushed the record button. "Paul, are you a Catholic?"

Paul started to laugh. "No. I have been asked that question before."

"There are probably going to be many questions you have been asked before. Please tell me if the questions are inappropriate."

"No, I am not a Catholic. In fact, I am not a member of any organized religion."

"Are you a Christian?" Bill held a short list of questions of a religious nature he had jotted down earlier at his office. He wanted to get them out of the way first, hoping the rest of the evening's conversation would be spontaneous.

"Yes, I follow the teachings of Christ." Paul watched the road ahead of him.

"But you are not a member of any one sect. Is that correct?" Bill turned sideways in his seat to be sure Paul's voice would be clear on the recording.

"That's correct. The people I administer to have little or no money. Most religions require money to keep up an image and add converts. I don't discourage any church membership but I don't promote any one sect. It is important that a person making a commitment to an organized religion be willing to live with the commitment. Most of the time, people live their religion according to their life rather than live their life according to their religion."

"Are you saying the world is full of hypocrites?"

"Hypocrisy is a natural human condition. I am saying if people lived their religions, well for one thing, no one would be without a home. Whether or not they choose to live in it is another matter. But no person on this earth would be without food, water or shelter if everyone practiced their religion."

Paul pulled off of the Terminal Island Freeway and down into an area of concrete bunkers, corrugated steel fences and railroad tracks. It was already seven-fifteen in the evening. A full moon was just starting to peek out from behind some scattered clouds. Paul parked the truck and Bill noticed several shadowy forms moving in their direction.

"Paul, your last name is Iscariot. Susan asked me if it was the same as the Iscariot in the New Testament." Bill kept an eye on the moving figures.

"Yes, there is a relationship. My family tree goes back to Judas. My full name is Paul Iscariot the seventy-fifth."

Bill knew his mouth was open, he could feel the dryness. He looked out the window seeing nothing but darkness. His thoughts were running like a racehorse.

Chapter 8
The Junkyard

"DO YOU MEAN TO say you are a direct descendent of the man that betrayed Jesus and you can trace your family tree back to Judas?" Bill was feeling the impact of his question. To his knowledge no one had been interviewed in modern times that showed a family tree back to the time of Jesus Christ.

"Bill, everyone can trace their beginning back to Jesus and beyond. How do you think you got here? Were your parents the first people on earth? Or their parents, or their parents before them? Haven't you ever thought about it?" Paul had an amused look on his face as he watched Bill's reaction.

"Sure, I've thought about it before but—"

Paul stopped him in mid sentence. "But you never went past your great-grandparents or maybe their parents?"

"I can only recall stories of my great, great-grandfather coming to California during the gold rush. He was an original forty-niner. He never made any real money in the north. He came down to Los Angeles in the 1860s looking for gold but never found any."

"I am sure if you traced your great, great-grandfather's family tree, you would find it traced back to Europe and beyond. Did any of your relatives come over with the explorers?"

"That's a good question. I have never really thought about it before." Several people stood around of the pickup truck waiting.

"You think about it, Bill. I need to speak with these people."

Bill looked at Paul as if he were in a daze. "May I join you?" Bill asked.

"Certainly. The people living here in the Junkyard are, by your standards, uncivilized."

Bill stopped him. "I spent two years in Vietnam reporting for the military. I know about uncivilized."

"You must have seen some very unsavory facts of life in those two years, Bill." Paul looked intently at Bill.

"Unsavory is putting it mildly, my friend. Not only did I see the ugliest side of humanity but the things I reported were often suppressed by the government. It seemed the only reports I wrote being shared with the American public were the ones giving justification to our involvement in South East Asia. I left the Army as soon as my tour was up."

"Did you do anything about it when you came home?" Paul asked.

"What could I do? I applied for a news job at NBC. During my interview I was told that any information regarding Vietnam was off-limits. There were network guidelines and so on and so on. I had a phone call from Washington before I was given the job at NBC. I was told the things I saw in Laos were government secrets and if I exposed any of the details regarding my experiences there, I would pay serious consequences."

"I asked about freedom of the press and was told government secrets are not freedom based. I was 24 and hungry for the job. I kept my mouth shut and lived happily ever after." Bill opened the door of the truck and stepped onto the ground.

"It sounds like you think you made the wrong decision." Paul reached across the truck seat and handed Bill a flashlight.

"This is in case of emergency. Don't shine it in anyone's

face. The people here are the faceless members of our society and they want to keep it that way. If they don't think you are here to arrest them or hassle them, they won't bother you."

"OK, no light in the faces. Can I talk with them?" Bill leaned back inside the truck and grabbed his sweatshirt.

"If the mood permits. Just listen for a while until they are comfortable with you. Then if the situation feels right. Go with your instincts, father/reporter. You understand."

Bill said softly to himself, "I'm not sure what I understand right now." He wanted to continue the discussion regarding Paul's family tree. He realized Paul had skillfully changed the subject.

There were a dozen men, women and children standing around the truck when Bill and Paul closed the truck doors. Paul spoke first. "Dell, are you here?" There was no response. Paul asked again, "Dell, if you're here talk with me."

The number of people coming toward the truck grew. A voice came from the darkness deeper than the gathering crowd. "I'm here, healer man. What you want?" The voice was low almost like an animal's growl.

"Come over to the truck lights where I can see you please, Dell." There was another long period of silence. Paul spoke in a low voice. Almost lower than Bill could hear.

"Dell is the self-appointed leader of the Junkyard. I always speak to him first in order to keep the peace. I don't think he would be violent, but men of leadership like to be recognized even this low on the chain of human existence." The bodies gathered directly in front of Paul began to part.

"Here I is, healer man." Dell stepped into the headlights. He was a black man, dressed in completely soiled clothing. His hair was in long dreadlock style braids and he had a dirty wool knit cap on the crown of his head. "What can old Dell do for you tonight?"

"I came to help the needy ones as usual, Dell. Is there anything I can do for you?"

Dell remained silent. He was looking at Bill Larkin. Dell had a handmade joint of what looked like marijuana between his lips. His eyes were glassy yet threatening.

"Who's the Lone Ranger got with him tonight? It sure don't look like Tonto!" Several of the crowd laughed out loud, others giggled.

"He's a reporter and a friend of mine. I brought him along to hear some of your stories. If you want to talk to him, his name is Bill."

Bill was surprised. He came along to tell the story of Paul Iscariot. Now he understood what Paul meant when he said it was a good idea to bring a recorder with him.

"I got nothin' to say to no reporter. You know how I feel about the outside world, healer man." Dell started to turn away.

Paul spoke. "He was in Vietnam. He was in Laos about the same time you were. Maybe you know him." Paul looked at Bill and nodded for him to speak.

"Were you in the Army, Dell?" Bill asked in a quiet tone.

"You sure weren't in no God damned Vietnam, reporter Bill. You talk like a pussy that's been lickin' cream out da bowl in the kitchen of some fine high-livin' home."

"Dell, I was in Laos 1964 and '65. Kind of off and on, reporting to the government what was going on out in front. I was moved around by a trained group of men called the 'Killer Rats.' They took me into tunnels, hid me in the jungle sometimes so close to enemy camps I could smell them take a piss." Bill made his point.

"Nam don't carry no weight here, reporter. Healer man, he can stay. Don't be in the Junkyard after midnight. There's some bad shit goin' down tonight." With that Dell turned and disappeared into the darkness.

"That was pleasant, Paul. Any more surprises in store for me tonight?" Bill looked tense.

"I am sure a seasoned reporter like you is rarely surprised. Pay attention and find the story here, Bill. We won't have any trouble now." Paul moved toward the first woman closest to him and asked her name.

"Janet."

"Are you sick, Janet?" Paul took her hand.

"I haven't had any good food lately and my stomach is hurtin' pretty bad. I been coughin' up blood sometimes." Her face was weathered. She looked about 50 maybe 55. Paul asked her how old she was.

"Twenty-eight or nine, I reckon."

Paul looked back at Bill, then back at Janet. Bill heard what she said and moved closer.

"Are you taking drugs, Janet?" Paul knew there was no healing the drug addicts. They had to kick the drugs before he helped them over their illnesses.

"No. I ain't got no money for drugs and I been off them for 'bout twenty-five or thirty days."

"You know why your stomach hurts, don't you, Janet?" Paul felt her forehead.

"Yes, sir. 'Cause I quit the drugs. My friend Sally said that you would help me if I got off the drugs and I just can't take the pain no more." She started to cry.

Paul held her hand. "I'll stop the pain in your stomach, Janet. I'll give you a note for the rescue mission in Long Beach. Do you have a child?" Paul placed the palm of his right hand on Janet's stomach and his left hand in the middle of her back.

"No, sir." She stood there with her eyes closed. She started to cry. "Healer man, my pain's gone."

Paul kept his hands where they were. "Janet, there is only one way for you to keep the pain away and you know what that is. You can't take drugs ever again."

"I know. That's what Sally said. She said that if I was to get off the drugs you would help me. I want to go home to see my mother."

"Where is your mother?" Paul asked as he removed his

hands and took a small card from his pocket.

"Ohio." Janet had stopped crying and tried to fix her hair.

"Where in Ohio?" Paul handed Janet the paper and put his hand on her shoulder.

"Cleveland."

"Do you remember her address?"

"Yes, sir. I have it written down and her telephone number too." Janet reached inside her pocket.

"You take this piece of paper to the mission. Ask for Gary Jenson, he is the minister at the mission home. Tell him I sent you. He will give you a hot meal and a place to sleep." Paul took Janet's hand and turned to Bill.

"Janet, this is Bill. He will take down your mother's address and phone number. I will be by the mission in a few days to check on you. If you stay clean and you're still at the mission, I will help you get home to your mother. Do we have a deal?"

"Yes, sir. God bless you, mister." Janet kissed his hand and walked toward Bill. Janet seemed to look her age again. He had seen a lot of things in his life but nothing this amazing.

For the next hour and a half Paul met with people one at a time. Often it was a woman with a child. Several men, younger than they looked, approached Paul. He spoke to them for a minute then sent them away.

If Paul touched one of those that came to him, he appeared to heal their illnesses. He gave each one a piece of paper and some instructions and then he would send them to Bill. Everyone had a different story. Some of them, like Janet, wanted Bill to contact their families. Others only wanted to tell their story.

Most of them were similar. Coming from broken homes, they had run away only to find life on the street impossible. Many of the homeless had turned to drugs and stealing. The women with any kind of looks had used prostitution as a way of earning money to buy drugs and what little food they needed to stay alive. It all boiled down to one thing. They did whatever it took to stay alive. Even if the life they had was worse than anyone could imagine, it was better than death.

Just before nine o'clock a large group of men and women moved through the shadows talking with several of the ones waiting to see Paul. After the meeting with Dell and Janet, Paul had turned off the truck's headlights. Using only the flashlights and candles Paul had brought with him made it hard to see much more than a few feet beyond where they sat. Bill could not tell how many homeless souls had passed through, but this last group was larger and moving quickly. Several of the men waiting to see Paul left with the large group. Paul stood up from the wooded box he was using as a seat and moved toward Bill.

"Several young men came by earlier and told me they were expecting a police raid tonight. The last group that came through here said the police have started at the north end of the yard and are moving south."

"One woman said there were as many as one hundred officers with dogs, using their nightsticks along with large metal flashlights to roust people from their hiding places and meager homesteads. I have been here before when the local police came through. They won't bother us." Paul turned off his flashlight and leaned against the truck.

"I know several of the officers from my visits to the mission. Believe it or not there are Los Angeles police officers who donate their time and talents to help out at the mission on their days off. You never read any of those stories in the paper or see them on the news. Let's wait here until the officers show up. I will ask if we can go along with them." Paul spoke softly.

Bill stood up and dusted his pants off with his hands. "Do you think the police will want us along after all of the bad press they have gotten lately?" Bill was not optimistic.

"I don't know how much exposure you have had lately to your local police but I don't think there will be any problems. Unless someone starts something, the police aren't out here to hurt these homeless souls. The woman saying the police had dogs and nightstick, I'll bet that is hearsay. The people living in the Junkyard don't have much fight in them. The only ones looking for trouble are the ones running from the law." Paul and Bill looked toward the wandering flashlights headed in their direction.

"Paul, is that you?" a voice came out of the dark.

"Yes, it's me. Who's there?" Paul asked.

"It's Chap. Dennis Chapman from the Harbor Division. How you doin'?" A large built police officer in uniform stepped out of the shadows. He extended his hand to Paul and shook it heartily. "I haven't seen you in quite awhile. Where have you been hiding?" Chap looked at Bill and let go of Paul's hand. "Who's this fella, one of your new converts?" Officer Chapman let out a loud laugh.

"No. Chap, this is Bill Larkin. Bill, Dennis Chapman, one of LAPD's finest."

"Knock it off, Iscariot. I'm not coming to your open house at the mission on Sunday. I have a full day planned with my son and a couple of his buddies. I'm taking them to Chino for paint ball wars."

Officer Chapman looked at Bill as though he recognized him. "You're a newsman, aren't you?" Chapman reached to shake Bill's hand.

"Guilty as charged." Bill took the officer's handshake.

"You were responsible for the story of our officer killed in the line of duty last year, weren't you?"

"Yes."

"That was a hell of a piece, Mr. Larkin. How'd you get tied into Iscariot? He talked you into going to the mission with him this weekend?"

"No, I just came along for the ride tonight. He wanted me to come to the Junkyard and possibly write a story about what these people go through living on the streets." Bill didn't want anyone to know about his personal involvement with Paul and his family.

"Well, you picked a fine fellow to hang around with. He is really something, isn't he?" Bill thought the word's 'fine fellow' was a definite understatement.

"Come on with us and see what we caught in the roundup tonight." Officer Chapman turned and followed the other officers passing through with several people already in handcuffs.

Bill and Paul started to follow. Bill reached for Paul's arm to stop him. "Does Chapman know how special you really are, Paul? Or does it seem everyone around here takes it for granted except me?"

Paul smiled. "The work I perform among the homeless is for the homeless. Most people wouldn't take what one of these poor souls said seriously if they took the time to listen. These people have a certain amount of pride in our relationship as well. Meaning that if they talk to someone on the outside, they violate an unwritten code among themselves. It is an interesting relationship to say the least. One that I cherish dearly and wouldn't change for the world."

They walked along in silence for a while lagging behind the police officers involved in the sweep. Bill's thoughts returned to the reason he had come with Paul in the first place.

"You were going to tell me about your family history. I asked you if you were related to Judas, the one, according to the Bible, who betrayed Jesus. Are you?"

Paul stopped walking and faced Bill. The full moon was shining so bright Bill could see Paul's face clearly. "Yes." Paul looked over Bill's shoulder at the moon.

"Would you care to elaborate on 'yes' just a little more." Bill was trying to keep from losing Paul's attention.

"The Iscariot family history has been passed down for generations. It is believed that Judas, after betraying Jesus and subsequently being forgiven by Him, dedicated his life and all of those coming after him to carry on in the footsteps of the Savior. My father taught me about faith and I believed him."

Paul looked at Bill and then at the moon.

"That's it? Your father. Paul Iscariot the seventy-fourth told you about faith and you believed him. That's all there is to it? Did he explain why you have not all been named Judas?"

"Yes." Paul turned and started to walk in the direction of the police.

"Well, what did he say?" Bill was showing some frustration.

"Judas, being ashamed of his own name, named his firstborn after the apostle Paul. The name has been passed on with the teachings."

"Then your son is Paul the seventy-sixth?" Bill reached for Paul's arm and stopped him again.

"One of my sons will be Paul the seventy-sixth. He will carry on after I am gone."

"How many sons do you have?"

"Three."

Bill stood close to Paul. He wanted to see his face clearly when he asked him his most important question. "Paul, did you bring my daughter back from the dead?"

Paul looked directly into Bill's eyes and then at the moon. Bill saw tears coming from Paul's eyes and run down his cheeks.

"Yes."

Bill started to cry as he took a step back. A voice came from deep in the shadows.

"Healer man. I need to see you." It was Dell's voice coming from behind Paul toward a corrugated fence.

Paul turned to look in his direction.

"It's my lady. She in real pain. Will you touch her?"

Paul stepped toward him. "I thought you didn't believe, Dell."

"I don't. But the lady, she does." Dell turned and went through a makeshift door made from one of the panels in the fence.

"Bill, you catch up with Chapman. I'll be right behind you."

A cloud drifted across the moon and Paul disappeared for a moment. When the cloud passed he was gone.

"OK, Paul, I'll be up with the police. Meet me up there. Paul, Paul?" There was no answer. Bill knew if anyone was safe here, it was Paul.

Chapter 9
Missing Person

BILL FOLLOWED THE FLASHLIGHT beams to the south until he could see a large navy blue bus parked under a streetlight. The bus had white letters on the side identifying it as belonging to the LAPD. There were thirty or forty police officers with at least fifty homeless people lined up against a steel fence. It was one of the fences surrounding one of the many automobile and truck graveyards being scrapped out for parts and metal. The entire four square block area was made up of car junkyards hence the name "Junkyard." The term was used by the locals, the police, the politicians and the people that lived there. Officer Chapman approached Bill twirling a nightstick.

"I heard you guys were cracking heads and using dogs in the sweep tonight." Bill motioned to the people lined up against the fence. "I don't see one dog or any bleeding heads."

"It's tough enough hauling all of the children of the dark into jail let alone to a hospital for treatment. Why, did you hope to witness some good old-fashioned police brutality?" Chap smiled.

"No, Officer Chapman, I have seen enough brutality in life thank you. I just thought..."

"You thought we would take advantage of a dark night with

no video cameras around and bust some heads?" Chap spanked the palm of his hand with his nightstick.

"It does seem like an ideal opportunity, Officer." Bill walked by him toward several people being searched.

"Are these people under arrest?" Bill asked.

"Yes, in violation of section 19934, trespassing on private property. That is the reason for the sweep. Of course in the process of the search of each upstanding citizen of the city junkyard we find drug paraphernalia, knives, ice picks and the ones with no money go down for vagrancy."

"What no guns?" Bill moved in for a closer look.

"Guns are worth too much money on the street. If one of these citizens is lucky enough to score a firearm, they cash it in for enough crack to last a month. If they had a gun when we moved through here, they hid it so they could come back and pick it up later." Chapman was standing close to Bill and giving him a blow-by-blow description of what was happening.

"Are they all handcuffed?" Bill asked.

"Only with nylon ties. Steel handcuffs are too hard to use in a mass arrest like this. Besides, the city can't afford to keep that many extra cuffs around."

Female officers searched the female prisoners and each arresting officer stood next to his or her prisoner for a photograph.

"What are the photos for?" Bill asked one of the female officers.

"They go in each plastic bag for each person arrested. That helps with identification and reporting later at the jail." The officer held up a small plastic bag. The kind with a Ziploc top about the size a sandwich would fit in.

"What all do you put inside the bag besides the picture?" Bill asked.

"All of their personal belongings," frowned the female officer.

"You mean, everything these people own is in that plastic

bag?" Bill couldn't believe it.

"Yep. Everything they have on them anyway. For example, this one has two dollars in change, a crack pipe, an unreadable ID card, one earring and a rubber. A used rubber at that." The female officer held the bag up to Bill's face.

Bill stepped back. "This is a lot compared to some of the people arrested tonight. Most of them just have a crack pipe and nothing else."

The female officer was asked to pose for a picture with the two women and man she had arrested. The officer with the camera spoke up. "Smile big now. This one is going home to Mama." The Polaroid flashed and a picture popped out.

"If this one is real good maybe you can use it on your Christmas card this year." The officer's sarcasm was wasted on the homeless but got a good chuckle from some of the other cops.

Officer Chapman tapped Bill on the leg and motioned for him to follow. Chap went to the other end of the bus. "Look at this little gal here. She doesn't even know where she is."

He was right. She was leaning with her back against the fence and her head so far forward her chin rested on her chest. Her legs were spread apart to keep herself from falling down.

Chapman continued. "I know this girl. She's been arrested several times here in the last three or four sweeps. Her father is a famous actor. I won't say because I promised him the first time she got picked up that I wouldn't give it to the papers. Her name's Tina. She left home at 18 and started dancing at a strip club in Hollywood. One night at a party for the special patrons she was given some crack to loosen her up. That was two years ago. She's only 23 years old and looks like an old lady. Her old man showed me some pictures of her. She was beautiful. What a waste."

He turned to look down the rest of the line of arrested individuals. "See those two guys with clean faces? One of them has on a baseball cap—you can still read what team it's from and the fellow next to him with the clean sneaks on. Those guys are long shore men. They have good jobs. One of them says he has a family and can't afford to go to jail. The other one is screaming he's on his lunch hour and needs to get back to work or he'll lose his job. They were taking turns with Tina for five bucks a pop. You tell me which ones are the scum." Chapman slapped the nightstick hard in his hand and walked away. He was right. How do you tell the good ones from the bad ones?

Another officer approached Bill and introduced himself. "Mr. Larkin. You probably don't remember me. I was one of the pallbearers at Officer Wilkerson's funeral. I introduced myself after the services and thanked you for your story on law enforcement officers killed in the line of duty."

"Yes. I remember you. You're Officer Reilly?" Bill was a good reporter. He saw Reilly's name tag when he approached and without looking at it again made the police officer feel as though he had remembered.

"You do remember. Mr. Larkin, I want to thank you again for what you did. It went a long way with the officers in the department."

"Yes, I have been told that several times. Glad to be of service. You guys have a tough job and with all of the mini cams around these days, you are always being judged by the public. Why don't you have any press out for this? It would seem like a good public relations opportunity. I haven't seen any brutality or excessive use of force tonight. You should call the station when you have your next sweep and I'll have a news crew here."

Reilly's expression changed. If Bill's comments were meant to be funny, he didn't see the humor in them. If they were serious, he was being insensitive.

"Mr. Larkin, do you have any idea how many arrests the Los Angeles Police make in a typical day? Thousands. Do you know how many result in police brutality? Usually none. Do you realize that for almost every criminal taken to a hospital for the treatment of injuries received during his or her arrest, two police officers are treated for injuries sustained while in the line of duty? Did you know all of these facts, Mr. Larkin?"

Bill was taken back by the officer's remarks to his casual observation.

"I suppose you feel that the officers were wrong in the Rodney King incident. In retrospect there was too much force used in the end to subdue Mr. King.

"However, you must take into consideration, police officers have only two options when they are stopping someone for breaking the law. One option is to give the order to stop. It is a simple order. Very explicit in its meaning. Stop means stop. If the person chooses not to obey that one simple command from a law enforcement officer then the officer must go to option number two."

"What is option number two, Officer Reilly?" Bill folded his arms and cocked his head to one side. Several officers gathered around the two men.

"The second option of a police officer in any situation where the person or persons in question fail to obey the first option is to enforce the first option. The simple fact being that any person deciding not to obey the command from a police officer to stop is capable of doing anything else. Including but not limited to pulling a gun and killing the police officer.

"If the officer is not obeyed on the order to stop then the person told to stop is going to do something other than stop. The officer then must be ready for the worst possible scenario. Officer Wilkerson gave the order to stop. But the perpetrator chose to do otherwise. Wilkey being white and the perp being black and all of this going down so soon after the King trial, Officer Wilkerson let down his guard and was killed in the line of duty!" Officer Reilly was shouting and when he said duty, he turned and walked away.

"Hey, man, don't mind Riles. He was Wilk's partner. He

gets real worked up over the brutality issue." The officer speaking was a black officer. He had his hand on Bill's shoulder. His name tag read Sgt. T. Wilson.

"I don't blame him, Sergeant Wilson. I could never do what you guys do every day. You carry a gun and face the possibility of death every time you stop someone. From what I have observed over my years as a reporter, it is usually some person that resents the fact you are in their face. Considering drugs and alcohol, I don't know how you men do it."

Bill walked in the direction of Officer Reilly. Maybe it was time to do a follow-up on police brutality and the brutality of the public.

It was nearly midnight when Bill checked his watch. He checked the recorder. The tape had run out. How long ago, Bill was not sure. He had not seen Paul for over an hour maybe two. He walked over to the opening in the rail yard where the street crossed the tracks and looked in the direction where he had last seen Paul. It was so dark, with the clouds covering the moon, Bill could not see past the light offered by the streetlamp above his head. Officer Chapman appeared out of the darkness in the direction Bill was staring.

"Officer Chapman, did you see Paul down there? I was wondering if he was headed back this way. The bus is leaving for the jail and I need to get back to Paul's truck."

"I spoke with him a few minutes ago. He asked me to take you back to his house so you can pick up your car. He gave me your cell phone and the spare battery."

Bill didn't understand. "He asked you to take me back for my car?" Bill looked beyond the officer into the darkness.

"Yes. I told him I didn't mind. I have to go to the jail first and finish booking procedures. Usually, in these sweeps, we pick up one or two felons with warrants out for their arrest. It won't take too long." Officer Chapman walked past Bill toward his car.

"He said it just like that? Take Bill back to his car?" Bill shined his flashlight into the dark and called Paul's name.

"Mr. Larkin, he won't answer you. I told you he asked me to take you with me. Sometimes he comes over to the jail after a sweep. Tonight he had something else to do. Don't worry, these people down here worship the man."

"I didn't think he was the kind of man looking to be worshiped." Bill turned off his flashlight and followed behind Chap.

"He doesn't. They just treat him that way. I've never met another man like him in all of my years working the streets. He really cares about the people. Not just any people—all people. If there were more like him they wouldn't need so many like me. So many police I mean."

"I know what you meant." Bill was still unnerved by being left by Paul.

The booking process took longer than Bill expected. By the time things wrapped up at the police station it was three a.m. Bill was exhausted. During the ride back to Paul's house Bill didn't speak a word. He was tired and confused. Dennis Chapman was tired as well. They arrived at Paul's around 3:45 in the morning. Bill's car was parked where he had left it. Paul's truck was not in the driveway. Bill got out and thanked Officer Chapman for the ride and waved good-bye. He unlocked his car and put his things in the passenger seat. He was still carrying the flashlight Paul had given him and thought about leaving it on the front porch.

After some consideration, he walked up the front steps looking for a place to leave it. He noticed there were no curtains on the front windows. He was sure there were curtains when he was here earlier. The front gate was open and so was the garage door. He took the flashlight and shined it through the front window. The house was vacant. Not one piece of furniture. Not a picture on the wall or a rug on the floor. Paul Iscariot and his family were gone.

Chapter 10
Who and What To Tell

BILL LARKIN ARRIVED AT his in-laws' house just as the sun was corning up. He had broken a back window in the Iscariot home and let himself in, looking for any clue that might give him a place to start looking for Paul and his family. There was nothing left inside the home. He searched the trash cans and found nothing. Even the trash had been taken.

"Looks like professional runners, nothing left but dust," Bill said thinking out loud. He went to his car and drove back to the Junkyard at 4 in the morning. It looked different now that he was alone. It was more ominous. Even knowing what he knew about the place and having spent most of the night with its inhabitants, he felt out of place and slightly afraid. He cruised as close as he dared, looking for any sign of Paul's truck or a place where he might be meeting with people. Anyone left in the Junkyard at this time of night was stoned or sleeping off a drunken stupor. If Bill didn't know better it would appear no one lived in the shadows or in the dark outline of crates and boxes making up the throwaway houses.

"If Paul wanted to be found he would be," he said to no one. Thinking about the last 48 hours made him feel as though the city of Los Angeles was more Paul's home than his own. *Los Angeles is a city of unique quality*, Bill thought as he reached back in his memory as though it were an episode of *This Is Your Life.*

Born in Long Beach in 1948, his father worked for Shell Oil as an executive manager of the old Wilmington refinery and his mother was a housewife. Growing up in an industrial setting allowed trips to the refinery as a boy along with his brother Stephen. Bill smiled as he remembered watching the oil wells pumping up and down looking like those old red felt birds bending endlessly over a glass of water. It was Grandpa Larkin's favorite Thanksgiving trick. He remembered how Stephen liked to stay close to home and close to their mother. Bill recalled his great explorations such as riding the Red Car after school. The old trolleys went from downtown Long Beach to Los Angeles, Pasadena, and several outlying cities. The entire area being called Los Angeles, made up of dozens of small cities spread out over a large geographical area. Bill relished the old football rivalries when lines were drawn by high-school boundaries and the fans that supported them. Bill thought about his college days as a semi football star at U.S.C. in downtown Los Angeles fighting it out with the Bruins in Westwood where the campus is surrounded by Beverly Hills, Brentwood, and Bel Air.

Similar to the Southern part of the United States, high school and college football teams seemed to be the points where lines between cities were drawn. After Vietnam and the seventies, those lines started to fade. One thing was for sure, Los Angeles as one large city had never been a great town for fan support. Fans from all over the world called LA home and Los Angeles fans only support the winners. If a team is losing even in a tight game, the fans leave the venue and head for the freeways. Bill was constantly amazed at this phenomenon. *It is more important to get home and see the ten o'clock news than it is to see if Barry Bonds can hit a game winning home run in the bottom of the ninth*, Bill thought as he shook his head and continued to search the dark. The nineties proved Los Angeles couldn't even keep a professional football team in business. Returning home from the war in Vietnam was a real eye opener for Bill. Los Angeles had become a city of cities. There were communities, pockets of people calling themselves a town or city disassociated with downtown.

Bill talked out loud to himself again. "It's as if no one lives in Los Angeles. LA has turned into a place to work or drive through on your way to one amusement or another." His face grew serious as he looked at himself in the dimly it rearview mirror. Turning his thoughts to his early experiences in journalism as he graduated from college and went to work for Uncle Sam, working on 'Need to Know' policies only and reporting what the government wanted its fighting men to hear in Europe and South East Asia, he felt some regret about his compliance to military directives but was rewarded on his return home. Ultimately landing a job at KBLA had been his reward and he knew it. The whole damn world had changed, specially Los Angeles, and he sat in his car realizing he had never reacquainted himself with the city he called home.

Bill marveled at the fact he was sitting in front of his in-laws' home as he turned off the engine of his Lexus. He shook his head and rubbed his face with his hands.

"How in the hell did I wind up back here?" he asked himself. He let himself in through the front door with a key from the flower pot to the side of the porch. Exhausted, Bill climbed into bed after a brief shower.

Susan put her arms around his neck. "What time is it?" she asked.

"Nearly seven. I'm sorry I woke you, Susan." Bill kissed her mouth lightly and put his arms around her.

"I was barely asleep, sweetheart. I have been waiting to hear your car come up the driveway. I dozed off until I heard the shower running. I'll pull the blackout curtains and leave a note for Dad. We can sleep as late as you like. Then you can tell me what happened over lunch."

Bill's eyes were already closing. His arms relaxed as Susan kissed him back. By the time she returned to the bed, he was sound asleep.

When Bill finally awoke he looked at the clock. It was after one on Sunday afternoon. Susan was not in bed and there was no noise in the bathroom. The room was dark except for the dim bluish glow from the digital numbers on the radio clock face. Bill lay there looking toward the ceiling into near total darkness. He retraced his steps and words from the night before wondering if he would ever see Paul Iscariot again. The door to the bedroom opened and Adrian peeked her little head, full of golden blond hair, around the edge of the door.

"Hi, baby girl. Come give Daddy a big hug and a kiss." Bill extended his arms and Adrian let the door close as she entered. The room went dark again.

"Daddy, where are you? I can't see."

"Just come straight ahead the way you were walking. Walk slow until you feel the edge of the bed. I'll be here to take your hand." Bill could hear her breathing getting closer.

"That's right, baby, just a little closer." Bill felt her small hand touch his arm. He put his hands around her waist and lifted her onto the bed. As he did, he moved over just enough to give Adrian room to lie next to him on the covers. He embraced her. In the dark his sense of smell and touch were heightened. Adrian kissed his cheek and put her hands on his face. Her breath smelled like sweet milk and cereal. Her skin and hair smelled like coconut and peaches. He held her for a long moment. In the dark she could not see his tears.

"Daddy, I missed you. Are you doing good?" Adrian felt a tear on his cheek and wiped it away with her hand. "Are you crying, Daddy?" She wiped another tear away.

"Yes, baby, but not because I'm sad. I am very happy. I am very happy you are here with Mommy and your brothers."

"How about Grandpa Jack and Grandma?" Adrian took her father's hand and held it to her face so Bill could feel her tears also.

106

"Yes, baby girl, I am happy to be with Grandpa and Grandma too." He felt her wet cheek and held her to his chest. "I am crying because I am happy too, Daddy."

Adrian and Bill lay in silence. Bill was thinking about how much she had grown in the last year. His thoughts drifted and he pictured her as a young woman and then as someone's wife. He realized that if it had not been for Paul Iscariot, he would be holding only a memory.

The door opened and Susan was standing there framed in sunlight from the large picture glass window behind her. "Good afternoon, Mr. Larkin, Miss Larkin, I think it's time to let some of today's wonderful sunshine into this room." Susan reached the blind and curtain strings before the door closed and turned the room dark again. She pulled the blackout curtains first and then adjusted the blinds so the light was not too bright. It was truly a brilliant day. She looked down at the bed and saw Adrian sitting up and patting the edge of the bed. Bill moved over making room for both mother and daughter next to him.

"Am I interrupting a private conversation?" Susan looked at Bill.

"No, not at all. Consider yourself joining one of those special moments that comes along to remind you what life is all about." Bill, Susan and Adrian hugged and kissed each other.

"Adrian, would you like to go help Grandpa make Daddy a fruit salad with fresh fruit from Grandpa's garden?" Adrian sat up. Her hair had fallen forward covering her entire face. They all laughed. Bill pulled her close again and hugged her tightly.

"Yes, Mommy, I'll go. After lunch, will you and Daddy tell me what happened with the stranger last night?"

Bill sat up and put Adrian in his lap. "Adrian, how about I tell you about the stranger right now before you go help Grandpa?"

"OK, Daddy." Adrian sat up straight and took Bill's hand.

"First of all he asked me to tell you hello. His name is Paul and he is a very nice man. He helps lots of people with their troubles and worries."

"Is that all he does, Daddy?" Adrian was very serious.

"No, he is a carpenter and kind of an all-around handyman as far as I can tell." Bill realized he had not asked Paul what he did when he was not helping people.

"Did he pray for me, Mommy?"

Susan looked through her tears. "Yes, sweetheart." She pulled Adrian to her lap and kissed her on the forehead, cheek and chin.

Bill took Adrian's hand and asked her a question. "Adrian, do you remember anything that happened that day?"

"Some things I can remember." She looked as though she was looking outside for an answer.

"You don't have to talk about it if you don't want to. I just wanted to ask what you remember about the stranger, I mean Paul."

"I don't remember what he looked like but I would know his face, I think." Adrian looked toward the sunlight coming in through the window.

"I remember a white light and then seeing Mommy holding me. I felt like I was floating in the air looking down on me and Mommy and some other men. Mommy was crying and so was the fireman. Then the stranger came up and took me in his arms. I can remember his voice but I don't remember what he said. His voice was gentle and he said things so quiet. I can remember his voice." Adrian looked so peaceful and thoughtful. She started to smile and then cry.

"I opened my eyes and Mommy was looking at me and started kissing me and crying really hard. Mommy grabbed me and hugged me tight and I looked for the stranger but he was gone."

"Is he God, Daddy? Billy said maybe he is God or something."

Bill looked at Susan and then at Adrian. "No, sweetheart, he is not God. He believes very strongly about God." Bill did not know what else to say. "Paul said he has more than just faith."

"Do you believe in God, Daddy?"

Bill could not find the words. Susan came to his rescue. "Adrian, it isn't that Daddy doesn't believe. Aunt Anita and Uncle Wally are Christians and when Mommy was little I went to church with them. Daddy didn't go to church when he was little. Going to church is how a person finds faith and without faith it is hard to understand God."

"So Daddy doesn't understand God?" Adrian was quick and very practical.

"Sweetheart, it is a little more complicated than that. It depends on a person's faith because God is someone you have to believe in even if you can't see Him. Does that make any sense?" Susan felt as if she was talking herself into a corner. Bill looked at her half amused and completely in love.

Adrian slid off the bed and headed for the door. She turned toward her parents just before she opened the door. "It sort of makes sense and it sort of doesn't. I guess it is one of those things you and Daddy are going to have to decide and then get back to me about." She opened the door and left the room.

Bill and Susan looked at each other and laughed. "Kids," they said together.

Susan pushed Bill to the mattress and kissed him. "What are we going to do? Being a parent is like exploring an uncharted ocean. You never know what to expect and just when you think you do the unexpected happens. The boys are asking questions about what happened and I am sure Adrian is talking to Dad about it."

Bill got out of bed and headed for the bathroom. "I am sure you will think of the right thing to say when the time comes."

Susan went after him. "Not so fast, mister. You aren't going to put this whole thing on me. I don't know what to say. I need your help. It's hard enough being a parent handling the day-to-day stuff. But this. I don't know where to begin."

"You have already begun." Bill turned and kissed Susan. "You are a great mother, Susan. I could not imagine anyone being a better one. As for what to do regarding Friday afternoon, well, I don't know what to say about it either. My gut feeling is to take it one day and one question at a time. When the children ask a specific question, we will answer it. If we don't have the answer we'll find one. Between the two of us I am sure we can handle it. That is the way we have worked it in the past, so I say we keep on doing the same thing."

"I am sure you are right, honey. I just don't want the kids to feel like we are keeping something from them."

"After I shower and shave, we can go into the kitchen and I will tell everyone what happened last night. I am sure the boys will be excited about the part regarding the police and the Junkyard."

Susan stood back. "What police and what junkyard?"

Bill smiled as he stepped into the streaming hot water. "I guess you will have to wait like everyone else and hear the story at the dining room table." He shut the shower door behind him and started singing a Sinatra ballad.

Susan went to the bedroom door and locked it. She undressed and got into the shower with her husband. "I don't think I can wait until the table conversation. You know how turned on I get when you tell one of your stories."

Bill took her in his arms and kissed her, telling her about the Junkyard and the events of the past evening. Susan put her hand to his mouth and opened the shower door. "I think we have company at the bedroom door." The water turned cold. "I also think we have worn out our welcome in the shower."

Turning off the water allowed them to hear the boys pounding on the bedroom door. "Hey, Dad, your lunch is ready."

Bill wrapped a towel around his waist and went to the door. As he opened it, the boys rushed in. He picked up Eric and gave him a hug then bent down to hug Billy.

"Can you guys wait until I get dressed? I have a story to tell you about the police and a giant junkyard full of old cars, trains and the stranger."

"Tell us now," both boys yelled.

"Give me ten more minutes and I will tell you the whole story. After the story, you guys can take me up the mountain on a hike. How does that sound?"

Billy and Eric frowned. "OK, Dad, but hurry." Billy grabbed Eric's arm and walked out of the room.

"Thanks, boys, I will be out in a few minutes."

Bill closed and locked the door again. Susan sat on the toilet seat and picked up the conversation where they left off. "Why do you think Paul left so suddenly? Do you think he is in danger?"

Bill was drying himself with a fresh white towel and stared off into the distance as he thought about her question. "No, I don't think he is in physical danger. I believe the experience with Adrian on the freeway was more public than he usually allows himself to become and there may be some fear of exposure. Have you seen anything in the news?"

Susan stood and dried Bill's back. "No more than bits and pieces about a mystery man healing or not healing a little girl after an accident on Friday afternoon. Without names and the people directly involved to interview, I guess the news has dropped the story. Isn't it hard to sell a news story on hearsay alone?"

Bill combed his hair as Susan put lotion on his back and arms. "More has been told about less. It all depends on the topic and its believability. If there is film and several eyewitnesses or the actual people involved in the story, you can sell it on television. The weaker or more unbelievable the story the farther down the chain of news it becomes, until it hits the tabloids or gets dropped all together.

"I guess Paul and his family are quite skilled when it comes to remaining invisible. He is so real and natural about the fact that he is someone special. It's just a matter of fact to him and the people close to him. Even the people who don't seem to believe in his power or faith seem to want to protect him. Like the fellow at the Junkyard. It is an amazing thing." Bill continued to get dressed. When he was finished, he took Susan into his arms and kissed her.

"Paul talked of his tremendous faith. He said he had sure knowledge of the truth about Jesus and his ability to heal. Being with him was like being in the presence of a perfect man. He is so gentle and kind, yet so natural. Like a regular guy and then not. Christ, it's hard to explain." Bill shook his head.

"Bill, maybe there isn't supposed to be an explanation. God is not one to perform miracles in order to impress people."

Bill stood back. "Except he allowed a miracle to be performed on our only daughter. When I asked Paul if he had given Adrian back her life, he said very plainly—yes. The miracle is anything but plain. Other than Bible stories I was told by my grandmother, I have never been exposed to faith or healing or anything like it. Now I have had a firsthand experience with my own family, my own daughter and wife and I don't know what to do or say or really even what to believe."

Susan spoke softly. "Do you believe in what Paul told you?"

"Yes."

"Do you believe what I have told you and that Adrian is here now, a whole person, alive to continue on growing into a woman?"

"Yes, of course I do."

"Then just let it go at that. If there is to be more to it, you will know it." They went into the bedroom and made the bed.

"Susan, I have been avoiding Stan Eversol like the plague. It has been almost 48 hours since the accident and he knows I am sitting on the story of a career. With Paul gone I have no reason to keep what I know quiet, except for the possibility of our family, and specially Adrian, becoming a circus attraction. I'll keep quiet for today but tomorrow is Monday and I will be at work."

Susan interrupted him. "Bill, you are one of the best

newsmen in the business. You are the best television news director in this city. You will know what to do and when to do it. Trust your instincts. I do. And remember, whatever happens, your wife and children love you, completely."

"I love you too, Susan. I will take your advice and let whatever happens, happen. After something so miraculous has touched our lives, I just don't want anyone to get hurt."

Arm and arm, they went to the kitchen where Jack, Elaine and the kids were waiting to hear about Bill's experience with the stranger. He told them. When he finished even the boys had tears in their eyes. Also by telling the story again, he knew what he had to do and what he would tell the public about Paul Iscariot the seventy-fifth.

Chapter 11
For the Love of Money

"MISS LEWIS, WHERE IS Larry Dawkins?" Thomas Rich spoke loudly into the phone intercom unit on his desk. "Miss Lewis, did you hear me? I asked why Mr. Dawkins is not in my office for our eight o'clock meeting. Miss Lewis, are you there?" Thomas's voice was without patience. "Jesus Christ, did everyone take the day off?"

He pushed back from his desk and hit his fist on the broad arm of his high backed leather chair. He stood and walked toward the large mahogany double doors that served as the main entrance to his office. Being almost seventy years of age had not slowed his step. Thomas strode across the floor as swiftly and with as much confidence as he had almost forty years earlier in the small but affluent offices on the top floor of the Los Angeles Petroleum Club. As he reached for the oversized solid brass door handles, the door on the right flew open, hitting the back of his right hand like a hammer blow. Thomas yelled and grabbed his hand.

"Thomas, I am sorry." Larry Dawkins stepped in behind the opening door. "Did you hurt your hand?"

Thomas squeezed his right hand with his left one. He was in obvious pain but tried not to show it. "You're damn right I hurt my hand. What in the hell do you think you are doing bursting in here like a damn barbarian? Besides, you are late, Mr. Dawkins." Thomas was waving his injured hand in Larry's face. He was so angry his face reddened with each hostile word from his lips to Larry Dawkins' face.

"I'm sorry, Thomas, it was an accident."

Larry hadn't lost any of his step either, despite the added weight, and like Thomas, he hadn't lost any of his hair. Although Larry was two years older, his hair had barely started to gray. A point that was a constant distraction for his longtime friend and employer. As the years worked on Thomas Rich so had his vanity.

"By my watch you are fifteen minutes late. Tardiness is still an unacceptable practice at the Thomas B. Rich Corporation or have you changed policy without my knowledge again?"

"No, sir. The policy is still the same. I would never change corporate policy without your approval, Mr. Rich. Please forgive me for being late."

Larry had changed company policy once in 1979. The son of a good friend of his had been killed in Vietnam and his name was to be placed on the V-shaped black marble wall to be known as The Vietnam Veterans Memorial in the nation's capital. Larry Dawkins and Thomas Rich had both gone to school with Jason Williams, although Thomas had never liked Jason. Larry and Jason were friends before Thomas had enrolled at Pepperdine University.

When Thomas found out about Larry's $5,000 dollar contribution for the memorial, which clearly violated company policy regarding gifts to charitable causes, he threatened to sever his business relationship as well as his friendship with L. W. Dawkins. It wasn't so much the fact that the cause was unworthy or the fact it was for Jason Williams; it was because he violated policy. In the eyes of Thomas B. Rich, company policy was everything.

Without strong commitment to company rules, an employee could not be trusted. Any employee not willing to dedicate his life to following the rules quickly became unemployed. It was a way to maintain control for Thomas Rich. A way to enforce his work ethic and keep all employer-employee relationships in black and white. Over the years it had cost the company many young hotshot college graduates. It had also saved millions of dollars in bad investments as well as Thomas's direct involvement with any of his employees.

In reality, Lawrence W. Dawkins was as much a part of the success of the corporation as Thomas Rich himself. After the incident, Larry realized Thomas could never fire him. He knew too much of the company history; the dealings and goings-on that could put not only himself and the company founder in prison for the rest of their lives but also other businessmen and politicians. After that day Larry started calling Mr. Rich Thomas but he made a point not to cross the line of policy change; company policy was law. Even though it was set by the CEO for his own personal reasons, they were also followed, to the letter, by the chief operating officer and the corporate president.

After an incredible shouting match between the two men, Larry had challenged Thomas to a fight. He told Thomas to his face, he was the biggest corporate asshole in the civilized world. Thomas stopped shouting and stood there for a long moment. He looked deep into Larry's eyes as though he were looking at his own reflection in a mirror. Larry would never forget what he said. *'Larry Dawkins for the first time in thirty years you called me Thomas. I think it should be that way from now on. You are, however, not allowed in this gymnasium without previous invitation.'* With those words Thomas turned and left the room. Larry called him Thomas from then on as he pleased. He collected his thoughts and returned to the current situation.

"Thomas, there was the most interesting article Miss Lewis was reading to me in the employee lounge. It was about—"

"You and Miss Lewis were sharing news in the kitchen?

You know the rules regarding fraternizing between employees on and off the job. What is happening to you, Larry? Is your memory slipping?" Thomas was serious. He was worried about their ages and from time to time he felt he was losing some of his memory or that his longtime associate was losing his.

"No, Thomas, I am clear on the rules of the company. But this article was about an accident on the I-5 freeway three days ago. A little girl was brought back to life by some stranger. After the incident he disappeared."

"That's preposterous, Dawkins. What paper was reporting such nonsense? The *Times*?"

"No, it was in one of the tabloids. You know the papers that always come up with those stories about you and some starlet or your questionable business dealings with other companies."

"You are losing your mind, Larry. I can't believe you would waste a minute on such gossip. You're turning into an old fool." Thomas sat down at his desk and started going through the file folder on top of the pile in front of him.

"The report was by a paramedic and several witnesses. It sounded as if it had real merit, Thomas. Do you realize what it would mean if it were true? If someone was walking around in this day and age with the power to raise the dead?" Larry was staring past Thomas through the window.

"I don't believe anyone has ever 'walked around' the earth with such a power. You know how I feel about such nonsense. I demand you drop this immediately. I can't understand, you of all people, believing a report written in a grocery store tabloid. Let's get down to business."

Larry turned away from the window and sat in his usual chair at a desk to the side of Thomas's. Thomas rubbed his hand and noticed the pain was still intense.

"First of all, I want you to make contact with the DeSalvo family in San Francisco and make a deal for all of the Rich Corporation malls in the San Fernando Valley. Richard DeSalvo has been after me to sell those elephants since the earthquake. It is in our best interest to sell now even if we realize a loss." Thomas continued to move through the stack of files on his desk.

Larry Dawkins removed his glasses and looked at Thomas. "After all the trouble we went through to keep those malls intact after the earthquake?"

"Mr. Dawkins, are you questioning my reasoning?" Thomas did not look up.

"No, Thomas, I was just wondering." Larry replaced his glasses and started writing on his notepad.

"Good. For a moment I thought you might be ready to break another rule."

"God forbid I should break another rule, Mr. Rich. God forbid." Larry was using a very sarcastic tone.

"Considering the $27,000,000 we cleared on the insurance payments by cutting the cost of repairs, I can't see how we can possibly lose, can you?" Thomas turned to Larry Dawkins. Larry shook his head and searched his computer phone book for a phone number. He found the DeSalvo Corporation number and dialed.

"Mr. DeSalvo please. This is Mr. Dawkins with the Thomas B. Rich Corporation. Yes, I will hold."

Larry clicked the mouse of his computer and the screen lit up with a colored pie graph showing the four largest malls in the valley. The largest being the Gallery with 35% of the pie. The Promenade, Fall Valley and Topanga Hills mall making up the 65% balance.

"Richard, Larry Dawkins here. How are you? Good, good. Yes, Mr. Rich is doing just grand, thank you. I will tell him you sent your regards. Richard, I am calling about your interest in the four San Fernando Valley malls owned by the Rich Corporation. Yes, yes that is correct. Yes, and the Topanga Hills being the fourth. He is ready to sell all four. You know their value better than we do, Richard. Your last offer was $110,000,000 for the lot. The earthquake damage has been completely repaired and all four malls are better than new. Pardon me? Yes, the value has gone up with the completion of the renovations. Yes, and all of the retrofitting to current earthquake standards has been accepted by the city of Los Angeles building department. All of the signed permits are here in the office. Pending your inspection correct. I will be available at your convenience."

"Larry, Larry." Thomas was trying to get his attention.

"Richard, if you have a moment, may I put you on hold? I need to check on one item. Thank you. I will be only a moment." Larry pushed the hold button and set the receiver down.

"Yes, sir, what is it?"

"Larry, I don't have time for inspections and meetings, etc. Just tell him I will take $150,000,000 cash today as is. He can fly down with the draft and see the buildings before he signs the trust deeds."

"Mr. Rich, with no disrespect, those buildings have been completely remodeled. Occupancy is averaging 95%. The value is closer to one hundred eighty-five, maybe two hundred million." Larry was astounded.

"I know that, you idiot. Get back on the phone and tell him what I want. He won't be able to resist."

Larry Dawkins hesitated.

"Do it, Dawkins. Now."

Thomas picked up his own phone and rang for Miss Lewis. "Miss Lewis, please contact President Demeril of Turkey. When his aide is on the line ask him to wait until I am on from this end and call me."

"Yes, Mr. Rich, right away." Miss Lewis activated the Video Telecomputer screen to the left of her desk. She typed in the numbers for the presidential aide, country of Turkey and pressed the send button.

As a gift to the President of Turkey, Thomas Rich had arranged for the installation of the most modern computer system and communication equipment available. The system was linked by fiber optic cable to the Rich Corporation Headquarters prior to the end of 1995. The gift was a gesture of gratitude for allowing the Thomas B. Rich Corporation to install and own the controlling interest in an underground pipeline extending from the Iraqi border to the Sea of Marmara in Istanbul. The pipeline's main product was oil. That was before Saddam Hussein attacked Kuwait.

Larry took a deep breath and continued shaking his head. He picked up the telephone receiver on his desk. "Richard, sorry to keep you holding. Mr. Rich wanted me to extend a special offer to you. The asking price for the mall package is $150,000,000. Yes, you heard me correctly. Yes. Yes. There is one minor catch. The transaction must be completed by the end of business today. A draft will be fine. My watch shows 9:45 a.m. Why don't we meet here after you have completed your tour of the properties. There is a heliport at each mall and one on the roof of our corporate headquarters. Yes, I think that would be fine, three forty-five. I will tell Mr. Rich. Yes and I will have the papers prepared for signatures when you arrive this afternoon. Yes, thank you, good-bye." Larry returned the phone to its cradle and turned toward Thomas.

"Well, that was easier than expected. I can't believe how eager he was to conclude the sale today." Larry removed his glasses and rubbed his eyes.

"Richard DeSalvo knows a bargain when he sees it." Thomas continued to open and close file folders on his desk as though nothing had happened. Thomas pushed down his intercom button. "Miss Lewis, as soon as possible, would you bring me an ice bag?"

Thomas was looking at a swollen black and purple mark half the size of a hardball on the back of his hand. Miss Lewis came through the doors with a bag of ice and a hand towel.

"Thomas, I truly am sorry about your hand. Is there anything I can do for it?" Larry stood and walked over to have a look at one of the hands that fed him.

"Nothing. I want to keep the swelling down so I can play tennis after the mall business is concluded." Thomas opened the drawer on his desk and took out some aspirin.

Larry turned toward the windows again and spoke. "Back to the mall transaction. You commented that Richard DeSalvo knows a deal when he sees one. I have observed over the years that Mr. Thomas Rich knows a deal when he sees one also. You realize there are several million dollars still on the table regarding this mall sale. I realize it also. Do you feel free to tell me what this is all about?"

Larry walked over to the bar at the west end of the office. He opened the refrigerator and took out some ice and orange juice. Putting both items in a medium-sized tumbler he put the cold items back in the refrigerator, cleaned the sink and returned to his chair.

"As president of the corporation in charge of real estate, you might as well know what I am about to do. However, the primary transaction taking place over the next two or three days involves oil and that is my specialty."

Miss Lewis' voice came over the intercom. "Mr. Rich, President Demirel's aide is on visual." Thomas turned in his chair to face the video monitor, opening the audio channel as he did so.

"Mr. Ozal, nice to see you again. Is President Demirel available?" Thomas straightened in his chair, buttoning his coat and tucking his tie. Thomas B. Rich has always been a master at presentation.

"Yes, Mr. Rich, the President has been looking forward to your call. I will tell him you are on now." Ozal spoke into a 1960 vintage intercom box on his desk.

Thomas thought, *Some things never change.*

"Mr. President, Mr. Rich is on the line. I am switching it to your station. Just one moment please." The aide signed off and clicked the mouse in his left hand sending all signals into the

President's office. Instantly President Demirel's face showed on the screen in front of Thomas.

"Mr. President, so nice to see you again. How are you feeling?"

"Fine thank you, Mr. Rich. I am constantly amazed at this wonderful equipment, allowing me to talk to you and see you at the same time. Besides yourself, the President of your country and a few of the other Western European leaders I never get to use it. How are you?"

"Doing very well, sir, thank you. Have you tried the new golf clubs I sent you?"

"Yes, I have. Thank you for the fine custom made bag also. Unfortunately none of it improved my game. It is fortunate I am not a betting man or I would have lost my presidency on the golf course." Both men laughed.

Thomas spoke first. "According to information made available to me recently, I understand we will be pumping oil through our pipelines by August of this year."

"Yes, Thomas, that is true. It has been very hard to face the poverty and subsequent criticism of my countrymen. Since Hussein failed in his idiotic plan to take Kuwait, we have had to sit on one of our most promising assets. I have been told the embargo on Iraqi oil will be lifted as soon as compliance with the NATO investigative team has been satisfied. It has been a long, hard wait. I inherited the liability from my predecessor and it has not been easy to say the least."

"I am sure the future will improve greatly as soon as the oil starts flowing. I am looking forward to the day. Since we completed construction on the pipelines they have yet to run at full capacity." Thomas leaned forward toward the screen.

He knew all too well the wait had been difficult; however, it had been a blessing. To show restraint in using the pipelines against NATO's wishes, they would now be rewarded for their patience. Thomas had made the most of the obstacle, taking credit in world meetings on petroleum and petroleum by-products. It had been a political football and the newly organized Rich Fuels Corporation was going to score a major victory.

"Your President assures me that our patience will pay off. Our reward is to have all oil pumped from Iraqi wells go through Turkey to the oil tankers waiting in the harbor. It will be a day of rejoicing for our people." The Turkish President spoke in a tone of true gratitude.

"That is the reason for my call, Mr. President. I would like to extend the amount of $60,000,000 to your government as an advance on future profits. Once the oil begins to flow there will be a tremendous amount of funds available for your people. This advance will give them and your leadership stability, until August. Let us call it an investment in our mutual success."

"Mr. Rich, your generosity is overwhelming. Thank you from the people of Turkey."

"No need to thank me, Mr. President. This is a sound investment in our future success. The money will be on loan until your cash flow improves. It will be payable over twelve months at a rate of 15%. Is that satisfactory?" Thomas knew how much President Demirel liked to bargain.

"Ten percent sounds more reasonable. Payable in say, six months after the oil starts leaving our country." President Demirel was looking forward to telling his countrymen about the available funds but salivating over the possibility of telling his close friends of his bargaining prowess.

"You drive a hard bargain, Mr. President. Would you consider 12% interest over a twelve-month period, if I make the funds available to you in the next 48 hours?"

"Yes, it is considered done. Mr. Rich, it is a pleasure doing business with you. I really must go now and attend to presidential duties. Will you handle the financial arrangements in the usual way?"

Thomas knew the Turkish President could hardly contain his desire to inform his ministers and start the wheels rolling toward public praise. He also relished the opportunity to start bragging as soon as possible. President Demirel had already stood and the screen Thomas was viewing showed only Demirel's stomach.

"Yes, Mr. President. It will all be handled electronically via computer with a report delivered to you by electronic mail. It is, as always, my pleasure. Please say hello to your lovely wife for me." Thomas sat back in his chair and breathed deeply.

"It is done. Good-bye, Thomas." With that, the screen went blank.

"Sixty million dollars. You are going to advance sixty million dollars to Turkey? In all of our years together I have rarely questioned you, Thomas. I have gone along with every plan, every method to carry out your plan and I have even crossed some major lines for you, my friend. But sixty million dollars to a nation neither you nor any other American has control over is irresponsible to our corporate policy. It is a bad investment. It's insane, Thomas."

Thomas Rich looked at Larry with a stern glare. "I told you a long time ago never to question my judgment. Over the years you have done it many times. Not in words but in your actions. If you didn't go along with one of my decisions, you checked it out every way possible without letting me know about your investigation. Was I always right?"

Thomas stood and faced the window. His back was to Larry.

"Always right? I'd have to say that is nearly impossible even for you, Thomas."

"Some of the little things may have tripped me up once in a while, but on the big issues, looking at the entire picture, haven't I been correct in the investments and in the people I chose to back or destroy? Come on, Dawk, look me in the eyes and tell me how wrong I have been all of these years." Thomas turned and looked directly at his only friend in life.

"In terms of business, I will say you are unbelievably right. My success financially has been tied to yours since day one. I thank you for that. In terms of human relationships and the way you have treated people, well let's just say your ends don't always justify the means. A lot of people have been hurt by you, or us for that matter when it comes to money. This thing with Turkey is different. You appear to be acting like some kind of a Kurd philanthropist. I can't imagine you giving a sixty-million-dollar advance to anyone, let alone an unstable republic in Eastern Europe." Larry caught himself getting ready to unload and knew it was too late for self-righteousness. He looked away from Thomas.

"Larry, in all the years we have spent cutting deals and people, you've never understood. It wasn't your place to understand. You were my greatest asset because you always did as you were told even if you felt that it was morally wrong. In fact, even if it was illegal. That is your gift, Lawrence W. Dawkins. My gift, on the other hand, is one of knowing. Knowing how far to push a person, how far to push a deal. Everyone has a limit, just like every deal has limit. Once you see how far that can take you and how far the competition is willing to go, you settle in. You decide what is worth the sacrifice. I have never found one God damn thing I won't sacrifice when it comes to getting what I want. Nothing. I have no ties but to you. I have kept myself free of relationships because I have wanted no weak points in my business dealings. Everything is expendable.

"Take the malls for example. I know on the outside it seems like an extremely risky proposition. In most cases it would be, but in this one case where $60,000,000 will bring returns of several hundred million, it is worth the risk. Even then the risk is truly minimal. Everyone from the President of the United States on down is involved. Leaders from every industrialized nation have a stake in the oil game. They all have their little slice of pie. The thing is, Larry, there is only one waiter. No one gets their pie until it is served to them by Rich Fuels Inc. This is without a doubt the biggest financial coups ever perpetrated on civilized man. Why don't we retire to the gymnasium and I will tell you why you are about to become more wealthy than you ever imagined." Thomas was too proud of his plan not to tell his only friend and shareholder. He pointed his right index finger toward Larry Dawkin's face, swollen hand and all. "But don't you ever question my judgment, or I swear on every fucking penny I have ever earned or taken, you will not live to remember the answer!" Thomas had stepped within striking distance of Larry's face. He was as serious as Larry had ever seen him. Thomas had been this vehement when he broke the unions in seventy-four.

Larry knew he was capable of destroying his only friend. It was the sole trait that had always separated them as men. He knew he could never hurt Thomas Rich. He also knew if money were involved, Thomas Rich could easily lift the first spade of dirt to cover the casket of Lawrence W. Dawkins and walk away without regret for sending him to his grave.

Chapter 12
How the Rich Get Richer

"MISS LEWIS, HOLD ALL calls until further instruction. Mr. Dawkins and I will be in the gymnasium. Thank you." Thomas motioned Larry to follow him through a side door of the suite into a custom gym and spa adjoining his office. It was top of the line. It had every piece of equipment imaginable, including; monitoring devices, aerobic equipment, weights, a two-lane lap pool, a one-tenth-mile running track around the perimeter, and a regulation size handball court. You name it and it was there. It was the largest complex in the Thomas B. Rich office tower. Complete with showers, steam bath, sauna, tennis partners and a masseuse on call. The tennis partners and any number of masseuses were female. Young beautiful women paid more than most executives and earning every cent.

Larry had stopped coming into the gym at his own discretion, several years earlier. In 1982, during the oil embargo, Larry questioned Thomas regarding dealings with the OPEC nations and the American owned oil companies. It ended in a fiery argument, which Larry lost and was told never to come in the gym unless he was invited. Now the only time he entered was when Thomas wanted to expound on the virtues of money, give him a lecture on the rules or have complete privacy. Thomas knew this arraignment bothered Larry

Dawkins, still he used the opportunity to show total control over his best friend's life.

Both men had lockers the size of the large walk-in closets, each containing its own bathroom and massage table. Larry missed the relaxation he used to enjoy here. But Thomas had been correct regarding the matter of OPEC and the oil companies and he would never accept the apology given by his friend. Both men dressed in shorts, nylon tank tops and cross training shoes. Larry's locker, clothes and personal belongings were just as he had left them only clean, as if he had just been there yesterday. It had been over a year since his last visit. Thomas started on a stair stepper for his warm-up exercise. Larry got on a treadmill and waited for Thomas to speak.

"By the year 2010, the six major oil refineries in the Los Angeles basin will be closed down. There will, however, be more automobiles and gasoline stations. And more jets coming and going out of seven major airports, heavy trucks hauling goods from the harbor to the rail yards in Los Angeles and more AM/PM's than in any place on earth. Fuel and oil related products will still be in demand. Who do you suppose will provide all of the gasoline, jet and diesel fuel? I'll tell you who, Rich Fuels Incorporated.

"Over the last week and a half, I have spoken with the heads of each of the six oil companies in Southern California. In order to comply with California's clean air requirements they have spent a combined total of four and a half billion dollars to upgrade their refineries. Next month all of them are going to raise their prices at the pump. The average increase per gallon will be thirty-five cents. At 72 million gallons a day in consumer purchases it increases the oil companies gross by one billion dollars a month. What other industry can make a return on capitol investment in less than a year? If you don't already know, Mr. Dawkins, the answer is none.

"The United States and the industrialized nations of Europe have given Hussein the green light for the exportation of oil.

Iraqi oil with drive oil prices down all over the world. By then the six majors will have recouped their investments in clean air and start packing for the Middle East, leaving only one company here to pump oil products from the tankers to the refineries for distribution.

"In August, 44 million gallons a day will be pumped through our pipelines in Turkey to the port of Istanbul on the Sea of Marmara. Tankers will be loaded and then distribute oil throughout Europe and North America. The largest portion coming to the United States. In almost every port the oil will be pumped to refineries via Rich Fuels Incorporated pipelines. Larry, by the year 2005, Rich Fuels will be the largest oil pipeline company in the world. I estimate profits in the range of twelve to fifteen million dollars a day. The stockholders of Rich Fuels will realize an annual profit in the neighborhood of $500,000,000."

Thomas bumped his injured hand on the back of a stair climbing machine. "God damn it," he yelled and covered his injured hand with his good one, trying to squeeze out the pain.

"I thought you and I were the only stockholders of Rich Fuels?"

Larry opened the ice box next to the water fountain and filled a plastic Ziploc bag with ice. He handed the bag to Thomas. Thomas placed the ice over his injured hand and sat in the seat of an exercise bike. Larry handed him a fresh white towel and Thomas wrapped it around the ice pack and his hand.

"We are the only stockholders of Rich Fuels, Larry." Thomas winced from the pain of something touching the back of his hand. He increased the pressure and increased the pain.

"My share of the stock equals 10 percent." Doing the math in his head, Larry took on the look of a man in a daze after seeing some marvelous vision. "I will be making fifty million dollars a year." He said it as though the words were coming from some distant cosmos.

"You were always good with numbers, Mr. Dawkins. Did

you ever imagine so many zeros?" The thought of his own share in Rich Fuels made Thomas forget the pain in his hand.

"You are a genius, Thomas. All of the times I kept my mouth shut and the few times I spoke out of turn regarding some of your business dealings, I never caught the vision. Now, after all these years, I see what you have been doing. That worthless property in all of those broken-down ports around the world. Investing our annual profits from the Thomas B. Rich Corporation year after year in seemingly valueless, idle pipeline installations, over fifty percent of which are still unused today. Sometimes it was all but impossible to keep quiet regarding what appeared to be the idiotic outlay of money I thought was partly mine. Not that I needed so much, but you know, what's mine is mine and so on."

"Silence has proven golden." Thomas peddled the Exerbike as he applied more pressure to his hand.

"The funds from the sale of the malls will be adequate to pay off their debt and satisfy my commitment to President Demirel. See to it as soon as your meeting with DeSalvo is concluded. Transfer all funds via our banks in the Grand Caymans and handle all transactions electronically. Have President Demirel sign for the loan. As has been the case with other foreign and domestic leaders, it is important he be a hero to his countrymen and indebted to me. Once the oil starts to pump through those pipelines, I want no delays or reconsideration on his part regarding our cash flow. Most importantly, you must complete all pipeline ownership and interests regarding the land containing those pipelines from our various holdings to Rich Fuels Incorporated."

Larry spoke up. "In heavens name, Thomas, if we move on all of the outstanding agreements involving oil and pipelines, it will leave our treasury almost penniless. I think—"

"You think what? After all of these years and the last hour of realizing my brilliance in 'The Art of the Deal' you are about to think? Dawkins, your reward for silence is 10% of 500 million dollars a year. Your reward in heaven, if there is such a place, would be far less. What will it be, Larry Dawkins, heaven or Thomas B. Rich?"

Larry shut off the treadmill and excused himself. After all, it wasn't like working for Scrooge. If he were ever to admit even a fraction of what he had done over the years to complete certain deals, he would spend the rest of his life in prison.

Larry showered and dressed in a fresh white shirt. Thomas always had new starched white shirts in the locker room. Even though Larry's visits to the gym had become rare, the closet contained at least a dozen shirts in his size and with his monogram.

"Is there anything else you would like me to do before I leave?" Larry asked. Not because he wanted to but it was part of the process of worship he knew Thomas Rich expected. "I need to get back the mall transaction so everything is ready when the DeSalvos arrive." Larry spoke humbly.

Thomas replied loudly. "I believe Laurie is the masseuse of the day. Call her and have her come in at 10:45. Tell her to shower when she gets here and address me at my table in the nude. I like it when she rubs me in the raw." Thomas flashed a smug grin.

Larry left the gym without speaking a word.

Chapter 13
The Healer, Live on Five

"WELL, IF IT ISN'T the mysterious Bill Larkin in the flesh. Where in the hell have you been all weekend and why the hell didn't you return my pages?" Stan Eversol was hot. His temper was legendary in the news industry. He was also known for his fairness. Bill's stomach was in a knot knowing he had pushed beyond fairness regarding the issue of the healer and Adrian.

"Stan, I had my pager turned off. It was impossible to call you and explain everything that happened. It was Susan and the children in the accident on Friday."

"Is Adrian all right? I was worried about your family as well as the story, Bill. You must know that. You think I don't understand family? Maybe you think I am all news, nothing but the news so help me God. Is that it? William Larkin, I am disappointed in your judgment. I really am disappointed."

Bill sat down in the chair across the desk from Stan. "Yes, Stan. Adrian is fine." Bill tried to continue.

"And Susan and the boys? Shit, Bill, we go back how many years, fourteen, fifteen this summer? What makes you think you can't trust me?" Stan was on his feet and coming around the desk looking for his cigars.

"Stan, it's not a matter of trust. I have never experienced anything like what has happened in the last three days. I thought I had seen it all. After Nam then Los Angeles for the last twenty years. According to all accounts Adrian was dead at the scene. A stranger comes along and prays for her and she gets up and walks. What am I supposed to do? As a father I'll be damned if I am going to let this thing turn into a sideshow with my family as stars. As a newsman I want to tell the story without prejudice. How can I do both?"

"Are you asking me or telling me?" Stan found his cigar box under a stack of files and pulled out a long Cuban. This was the last of a dozen boxes of not only illegal but rare Cuban cigars. They were a gift from Fidel Castro, in exchange for the unprecedented coverage of his last visit to the United States.

Castro had called Eversol because of his award-winning story on Trijulo Stevens' last amateur fight. Eversol gained a reputation for sports coverage during the sixties and seventies. He graduated to news director of KBLA in the mid-eighties on the heels of a mass senior management shake up. His first appointment went to Bill Larkin as his personal assistant. He was hard driving but practical and only reported what his news staff felt worthy. Unless they had missed the point of giving the public what they wanted. He knew the public wanted to hear about the stranger on the I-5 freeway. He also knew the story would require kid gloves because one of his people, his main person, was directly involved.

"Bill, I can see your dilemma, believe me. However, there is more than just a story here. In times like we are struggling through, as a society, a story like this, properly handled, provides hope. And more than hope it restores faith. Faith in mankind, faith in God."

"I didn't know you believed in God, Stan. The only time I have ever heard you refer to God in all of the years I have known you is when you ask him to damn something."

"Religion is a very personal thing, Bill boy, it's not something you talk about freely. The same as politics." Stan moved back behind his desk knowing he had opened the wrong can of worms.

"Politics, that's a laugher. You are the most vocal person on politics I have ever known. Don't try and snow me, Stan, I know you want this story and I know we have the scoop. I just don't know how to present it without getting my daughter involved and if I go to extremes protecting her from the other media hounds, they will cry foul. Since you are such a religious person, Stan Eversol, just how much heat can you withstand?" Bill reached under the pile of files and took out a Cuban for himself.

"Have a cigar, Bill. How thoughtless of me." Stan never shared his cigars with anyone.

"Thanks, I don't smoke." With that Bill broke the cigar in half and then half again.

"How did that feel, Stan? When I took it, you offered it to me even though it pained you to do so. When you saw me break it in half you almost passed out. This is only a cigar, my friend. It is valuable and hard to replace. Well, my daughter and family are one hell of a lot harder to replace than this damn cigar. I will give you a story, but not yet. I need another day to track our stranger and ask some questions." Bill put the four pieces of cigar on top of Stan's desk.

Stan was just regaining his voice. "You made your point, Bill. Did you have to ruin one of my last Cubans?"

"There isn't much you care about in this world, Stan. I didn't know how else to get to you on such short notice. Can Jane Turner run finals on the news for me the next twenty-four hours? She is doing a great job as my backup on evening news. I think she can handle it."

"Sure, sure. She can handle it. I can't believe you trashed my Cuban."

"Get over it, boss. Listen, I spent most of the night with the stranger Saturday and Sunday. He left me with the harbor cops and when I went back to his house he was gone."

"Gone? You mean as in packed and moved, gone?"

"Yes—lock, stock, and barrel." Bill stood in front of Stan's desk.

"When did you find out who he was? How did you find him so fast? We have been looking everywhere for a clue and—"

Bill broke in. "The tape."

Stan looked puzzled. "Oh, the missing sky cam tape. I should have known." Stan relaxed in his chair still looking at the quartered Cuban.

"Listen, Bill, I trust you. If you hadn't already found and interviewed this guy, I would have been disappointed. I knew you were on it. But a story like this can't wait forever. Someone else is going to find this guy. There is already a reward offered by the *Times* for any information regarding the whereabouts of the 'Healer.' I don't know if this man can heal or not, but the people are starting to swarm and they want to know. I'll give you 24 hours, do or die. I can't wait any longer." Stan took a deep draw on his cigar and fumbled with the broken pieces of the one in front of him.

"Take it from me, Stan, he can do more than heal. If I can find him, I will bring you the Pulitzer Prize for the new millennium. Thank you for the extra time."

"Hey, can this guy fix my cigar?" Stan held up the pieces, two in each hand.

"That's some religion you've got there, boss. At least in hell, you won't have to ask for a light!" Bill walked out letting the door stand open behind him.

The first place Bill stopped was his office. He picked up a blank notebook, some pens and a laptop computer. He grabbed the backpack he had in his office. He had bought the backpack for William Jr. as a birthday present, forgetting to bring it home on the night of the party. For months Bill kept moving it around his office trying to remember to put it in his car. Now he knew it would come in handy. Bill added some extra batteries for his cell phone. A 35 mm camera, a bottle of water, and some gum he kept in his desk. He wasn't sure why but it seemed like a good idea at the time.

His next stop was the office of Jane Turner.

"Jane, have a minute?" Bill closed the door behind him. "I need a favor."

"Sure, Bill, anything. How's Adrian?"

"How did you know it was Adrian?" Bill was stunned.

"The guard told me you were in late the other night. The reports I heard on the other channels were about a little girl and her mother on their way to a soccer match. You were on your way to meet your family at a soccer match. When I couldn't find the sky cam film of the accident, I figured it was your family. Eversol knows about it too, but no one else."

"I just left his office. He is giving me 24 hours to bring in the story the way I want it told. I asked him if you could stand in for me on the day and evening news. Do you mind?"

"Not at all, take the time you need." Jane stood and walked toward Bill.

"It is a lot to ask of you on such short notice. You can use Mike Wells as a backup. I think he will give you his best. And Adrian is fine. Thank you for asking."

"Are Susan and the boys OK?"

"Yes, everyone is well. Thank you, Jane. I have one more favor to ask."

"Anything, Bill, anything. What happened out there on the freeway?" Jane stood directly in front of her boss and looked in his eyes for a response.

"I need a camera crew and mobile unit on call. I need the best one we've got. If they're not together now I would like you to assemble them. Take them off whatever project they're on now and put them on standby. Can you do that for me?"

Jane did not lose eye contact. "That's a tough one, Bill. There are several hot stories on the street and we are spread all over the city. Can you be more specific on the time you will need them?"

"No."

"OK, you're the boss. I'll take care of it one way or another. Can you tell me what happened?" Jane put her hands on each

136

of Bill's arms. "It's true, isn't it? What they are saying."

Bill stepped back. "What who is saying?" Bill knew what she was asking but he would not let on until he was ready. "It's in one of this morning's tabloids. It says a little girl was brought back from the dead on the I-5 last Friday. It was Adrian and you know the man that did it, don't you?"

"Just have the camera crew ready and waiting for my call." Bill turned to go then stopped. "If it is really true and my first thoughts were that it was just a miraculous coincidence, then I will tell the story. If it is not the truth I'll bury it and let the tabloids work their magic of confusion. Yes, I have met the man. And if anyone could have performed a miracle it would be him. Are you positive no one else knows?"

"Yes, no one at our office has a clue." Jane embraced him and stood back. Bill opened the door and waved over his shoulder.

Jane got on the phone and started rounding up the best members of their mobile teams and the newest mobile unit. Once the team arrived, she called them into her office. She gave the three men and one woman what details they needed to know, which wasn't much more than they were to wait for a call from Bill Larkin.

"Make sure the mobile unit and all the equipment checks out prior to hitting the coffee room. I want all systems in green light condition or better. Wes, you make sure the van and backup car are fueled and motor pool gives them the once-over. Mark, you and Patricia check on extra film, batteries, leads, and most of all, the cameras and lenses. Maxwell, double, no triple check the satellite feed to the station and run an audio and video check for live feed. If what Bill Larkin thinks will happen, happens, we may only get one chance at this story. Any questions?"

Maxwell Dennison raised his hand. Patricia hit him in the ribs with her elbow.

"Hey, what's that for?" Max rubbed his rib cage.

"You're not in the fifth grade anymore, Maxi. Just ask your question without raising your hand. When you raise your hand it makes me feel like I have to, and I don't."

Max smiled as did the rest of the members of the crew.

"What is it, Max?" Max looked at Jane as though confused. "What is your question, Max, or did you forget already?"

Jane was amazed at the childish antics of such experts in the field of news and technology. She knew from her days in the field that acting childish often relieved crew members of the stress and pain felt after reporting on the ugliness of modern civilized man.

"My question. Yes." Max scratched his face and beard. "Oh yea, what's the boss expecting, an invasion from Mars?" Everyone laughed and threw paper balls and shot rubber bands at Max. All except Jane.

"Not hardly. Do you remember the accident on Friday? The one about the little girl on the I-5 freeway? Patricia, you remember. You and I were looking for the sky cam tape of the flyover."

"Yes, I remember. We were in a panic because Eversol wanted coverage and we had nothing. Why?" Each member of the team looked intently at Jane for the answer.

"The boss knows who the little girl is." Jane stopped short. "And the boss has the guy they say healed her. Jesus, what a scoop."

The crew high-five'd each other and yelled, "High-five, still top of the heap."

"Chill, little ones, there is no story yet. At least no confirmation. Keep it under your hats and wait for the call from the boss. Remember, not a word to anyone."

Jane dismissed them and stood behind her desk. She picked up the receiver of her telephone and dialed. The phone rang three times before it was answered. "Hello, this is Jane Turner, may I speak with Larry Dawkins please? Yes, I will hold."

Chapter 14
Dell's Lesson

THE CLOCK IN THE car read 9:06 a.m. It was Monday morning and Bill had already filled the tank with gas and loaded the gear he thought he might need for his search. He did not know where or how long his search would take him. In his gut he felt helpless. There were many questions he had to ask Paul Iscariot before he could put his story on the news. Telling Stan he had a Pulitzer on his hands had been a lie. Maybe he did, maybe he didn't. In Bill Larkin's mind he had not decided to tell the story at all. He only knew he had to find out more. Susan agreed to stay with her folks another day or two. No one had tracked them down. Bill knew if they could stay secluded for a few more days it might blow over. The only report he had heard since the sketchy television broadcast on Friday evening was the one tabloid and the story sounded typical of tabloid press.

His first stop would be the Junkyard. During the day he figured he could find Dell and offer him some cash for the whereabouts of Paul Iscariot. He exited the Terminal Island Freeway just as he and Paul had on Saturday night. There was a low, thick layer of smoke and fog hanging just above the ground. It moved through the openings of the Junkyard like a long, man-eating snake. Everything looked gray and smelled like oil mixed in water. There were little fires dying out after burning all night, their attendants passing out from the wine or crack they ingested.

The entire area had been barricaded by concrete divider walls like the ones used during freeway construction. Parking the car presented the first problem. The only place that looked safe was in front of one of the junkyard offices used to buy and sell scrap. There were several mangy dogs sitting and traipsing around in and out of an open gate. Several Hispanic men and one black man stood in front of the gate as if they were waiting for something. Broken glass and metal fragments littered the ground and made Bill consider his tires and how long it would take to fix if he got more than one flat. He wondered if Paul considered these kinds of things when he visited places like the junkyard. Probably not. Bill parked his car between the dogs and the workers as close to the gate as possible.

The black man walked toward him. "Hey, missa, you can't park no car like that here. Where do you think you is—Bevly His?"

"No, I know where I am and I know who I am looking for. Who wants to earn ten bucks to keep an eye on my car?" Bill's directness made the Mexican men look away. But the black man kept coming toward Bill.

"Lester. He da man for da job. You give ol' Lester dat ten-dollar bill and he watch real good. I won't even let no dog piss on your tires."

"All right, Lester, here is your ten. When I come back, if the car is still here with all of its parts, I will give you another ten. Do we have a deal?"

Lester exposed a toothless grin with a pile of wet tobacco oozing from some deep pocket in his mouth. "Who you lookin' for?" Lester snapped the ten-dollar bill and held it up to the sun.

"I'm looking for Dell." Bill noticed Lester turn almost pale. "Why? You know Dell?" Bill asked.

"Me, no I don't know no Dell, real good that is. Does he know you comin'?" Lester shoved the ten-dollar bill deep into his overly soiled pants pockets.

"Not exactly. I need his help finding a friend."

Lester held out his hand. "White man, you better pay me the other ten dollars right now 'cause you won't be back to get yo car. I can guarantee dat. Yo, Jose, you hear this white man? He gonna see Dell. And Dell don't know he comin'."

Bill took the backpack and locked the car. "I'll worry about Dell and whether or not I am coming back. You just worry about the car or I'll ask Dell to talk to you directly."

Bill turned and walked along the railroad tracks into the hanging gloom. He disappeared after less than fifty feet. When he turned to see if Lester was still next to his car, he could see nothing but gray.

Bill Larkin walked a few hundred yards to where he figured he had seen Paul just before he vanished. The only sounds he could hear were the occasional deep tar coughs of someone that slept in the cold damp air night after night. He wondered what it was like to wake up without a bed or a bathroom. How many days could a person keep living like this before nothing mattered anymore? Drugs and alcohol were the answers. Once you're this wasted, you don't care where you wake up.

He was about where he last remembered seeing Paul. He walked toward the fence and felt along the sections of metal trying to find one that would open. He kicked at the bottoms with the toe of his right shoe and hit his fist at the tops trying to find a loose one. Suddenly a panel pushed in at the same time two arms grabbed him around the throat. He was blinded by fear and the rancid sleeve of an old wool navy coat. The sleeve smelled like piss and puke. It covered his eyes, nose and mouth. Bill fought to get a breath but the arms tightened until he felt he was passing out. He stopped fighting. A mouth came up to his ear and touched its lips to the soft skin on his ear lobe. He felt the wetness of a tongue slide along the outside edge of his ear and then his ear was between a pair of teeth as if they were going to bite it off.

"What you doin' here alone, reporter man?" Bill recognized Dell's low growling voice. At the same time the sleeve across his mouth moved so he could answer.

"I need help finding Paul. I can pay for the information." Dell laughed loud in Bill's ear. He laughed so loud Bill felt the pain of a headache coming on almost instantly.

"If you got the money on you, I can take it off your dead body." He felt Dell's grip uncoil. He started to pull away causing Dell to re-tighten his grip.

"Listen, white bread, you don't move until I say you can move. You hear me?" Dell squeezed his neck so the air could not pass in or out. Bill nodded. Dell relaxed his grip and used one hand to search for Bill's wallet.

"Well, well, what have we here? Looks like hundreds and twenties. How much, reporter man? How much you think you have to give of Dell to tell you where Healer is?"

"All of it if necessary." Dell tightened his grip around Bill's throat.

"Oh, you gonna give it all to Dell, every fuckin' dollar." Dell released Bill and kicked him in the back hard enough to send him into the steel fence cutting his forehead. Bill turned to face Dell and saw he wasn't alone.

"You're Dell's woman, aren't you?" She nodded slowly and Dell hit Bill in the mouth. Blood trickled slowly from the corner of his right lip.

"Shut your mouth, white bread. No one talks to my lady less I say so." Dell continued to count the bills he had taken from the wallet.

"The healer was here two nights ago, did he help you?" Bill was looking directly at the woman. Dell hit him again.

"Don't you hear good?" Dell slapped him.

"One thing for shor', white bread, he ain't here to help you."

"Listen, Dell, do what you want to me and keep the God

damned money but Paul is in danger. His family is in danger. There are people looking for him. I can help." Bill wiped the blood from his chin and looked at Dell.

"Healer man can take care of hisself. He don't need yo help. 'Sides, I don't know where he at. Never have. He comes and he goes just like that. Nobody asks, nobody cares." Dell fanned the cash in front of Bill Larkin's face.

"He can't take care of himself this time. What he did for my daughter wasn't hidden in some junkyard or back alley. It was in plain view in the middle of the day on the I-5 freeway. There are pictures of him and his truck. That's how I found him. Someone else will too. There's no telling what could happen once he is out in the open. His work, all the people he helps will be lost. Nobody gives a shit if you people down here live or die except Paul. You know and I know he is special and he needs my help. Tell me where he is, Dell. Do this one decent thing in your life and help the man that helped your woman." Dell raised his arm and Bill covered his face.

"Here yo wallet, white bread. I put the money back. I can't tell yo where to find the healer but I know someone that can." Dell reached inside his coat pocket and pulled out a card. It was like the cards Paul was handing out the night of their visit. It had Gary Jenson's name and the address of the Long Beach Rescue Mission. Bill took two one hundred dollar bills from his wallet and gave them to Dell.

"Amazin' ain't it, white bread? You figure yo life worth two hundret dolla. Healer man put no price on life. Get yo white ass outa my yard and don't come back unless yo wit him." Dell pushed Bill hard in the chest and he fell back through the fence onto the railroad tracks. His backpack came flying after him and landed on his stomach. He got up and walked back to his car. His head and mouth hurt but he was alive and he knew why.

Lester was sitting on the hood of Bill's Lexus and he could hear the scratch as Lester slid off to the ground.

"Hey, white man, you bleedin'. Yo musta found ol' Dell. I tol yo not to go down yonder. You don't look so good." Bill stood straight up and acted as if he could kick ass if he needed to. Lester stood back and dusted off the deep scratch he put in the hood.

"Here's your ten, Lester. Now go away."

Bill unlocked the car and fell into the seat. His head was pounding and his chest hurt. He started the car and drove toward the freeway. Once he was out of the junkyard, he pulled over near a sign that read, 'Never Closes' and parked the car. He went through the front door of a well-known waterfront bar. Well known for cheap whisky and even cheaper women. He was greeted with the music of the sixties blaring from an old jukebox in the corner. He put twenty dollars on the bar and ordered a whisky straight. He walked to the back and into a filthy men's room. It had no switch for the light, but a thin chain hung down from the ceiling and he pulled it. The light blasted his eyes and the dirty mirror revealed the source of his pain. His lip was bleeding as was his right ear. Blood also trickled down the side of his head. He felt lucky to be alive. The faucet worked but barely. He washed his hands with an old bar of lava soap then cupped them to wash his face. The cool water felt good. He reached in his pocket for a bottle of Excedrin and took four, putting them in his mouth as he turned off the water. He walked back to the bar and picked up the drink. He downed it along with the Excedrin and set the glass down hard on the wood bar top.

"Another." The bartender's sleepy eyes never moved as he poured another glass of cheap whisky for his bleeding patron. Bill downed it and slid the rest of the twenty-dollar bill toward the bartender.

"Keep the change." Bill walked back out the way he had come in; into the gray stench of the harbor on a cold January morning. He retrieved his Thomas Guide from the trunk and sat in the driver's seat. Pulling down the visor and opening the lighted mirror, Bill took some of the first aid supplies from the glove box and his backpack. He treated the cut on his face first with antiseptic and then with a clean piece of gauze. The blood stopped flowing and the pain soon gave into the Excedrin he had taken with his first shot of whisky.

Bill winced at the pain in his chest region and wondered if he had broken a rib or two. Flashing back to Nam made him remember the pain of broken ribs and he realized this pain was not that intense. He opened his shirt and daubed a piece of gauze with peroxide on his scraped skin just as a precaution.

"Looks like I've slowed down a few steps. Ten years ago I could have taken out Dell before he got a chance to hit me in the face." Bill spoke out loud as he moved his attention to the upper swollen lip Dell had given him. He held a folded piece of gauze over it and squeezed. Blood came gushing out and down his shirt like it had when he was first hit. He dabbed at it as well and when the bleeding stopped, he put a butterfly bandage on it with some antiseptic salve from a tube in the first aid kit. Once the booze and Excedrin started to work, he felt good enough to drive. Bill fished for the card Dell had given him and found the address location on his map. The Long Beach Mission was only a block off Ocean and in a section that had seen some better days. However, the evidence of the Long Beach cleanup campaign was showing a great improvement. Bill walked up the steps slowly and through the front door.

The mission was a restored hotel that had served as a church during World War II. The Navy made it a home away from home for the sailors coming into port on leave. Not all of the sailors were looking for cheap wine and whores. The old Mira Mar Shores was made up just like a place mama would have lived in. One of the local churches bought it from the Navy after the war and used it as a place for rail, oil workers, and transients to call home as long as they made some contribution to the collection plate or helped keep the place in repair.

A tall man in a dark overcoat, black T-shirt and black jeans walked out of a side door into the main hallway when Bill's footsteps announced his presence.

"May I help you?" The man looked at Bill's face. "Oh, you're hurt, come in here, you poor man. What happened? Were you mugged?" The man removed his coat and pulled a white smock on over his T-shirt. He took Bill into a room that looked like a small emergency room in a country hospital. There was a stainless steel table on wheels, two or three chairs and a large cabinet covering one wall floor to ceiling with a framed glass door.

"In a way, I was mugged. However, instead of my mugger stealing my wallet, I paid him when he gave it back."

The man turned away from an open drawer he was in, searching for iodine and bandages and looked over the top of his split glasses at his patient. "That's a new one on me. I can't say I have had many souls in here that have paid their way out after a mugging. You look like you got mugged in spite of the payment. Your clothes don't look like you slept on the street last night. Are you a local?"

"No not really. I was born and raised in this area but I moved to the Valley when I was a teenager." Bill felt like a kid in the school nurse's office. "You must be Gary Jenson. My name is Bill Larkin."

Gary turned completely around this time and took a long look at his patient. After a moment he turned toward the counter again and cleared his throat. "You're the reporter I heard about yesterday."

Bill looked puzzled for a moment and then smiled. "So you have seen Paul Iscariot. He is the only one that would have told you about me."

"Not necessarily." Gary took the medical supplies he had put on a tray and walked toward the table. "Would you please sit up on the table and I will dress the cuts on your face."

Bill did as he was asked. "Who else would have known I was a reporter and had a reason to tell you I had been down in this area Saturday night?"

"Lots of people. There is a very small community circulating in and out of the mission. It could have been any one of several women and children coming in here for assistance from the Junkyard. That is where you were the other night, was it not?"

"Yes, and more recently than that I'm afraid." Bill rubbed his chest and asked for a glass of water. "I had a run-in with Dell this morning."

Gary handed Bill a glass of water. "Kind of early to look for trouble, isn't it?" Gary Jenson had a tone of sarcasm in his voice and pressed the cut on Bill's forehead and rubbed out the dirt.

"Ouch, that hurts like hell. Can you be a little easy on the wiping?"

"Sorry." Gary showed a faint smile.

"I wasn't looking for trouble. I am looking for Paul Iscariot. Do you know where I can find him? It is extremely important."

Minister Jenson looked skeptical. "It must be important if you would risk your life to find him. How did you run into Dell?"

"You know Dell, he more or less ran into me. That's how I got your card. Dell gave it to me after he gave me back my wallet."

Gary's skepticism increased. "Dell took your wallet and gave it back. You must have a guardian angel."

"No, that would be my daughter Adrian. Paul was her guardian angel last Friday afternoon."

"Yes, Paul told me. What do you want with him?" Gary finished his nursing and put the leftover supplies back in the cabinet.

"It is vital I see him at once. I think he is in danger. If not him personally then his mission."

"What do you know about his mission?" Gary led him into his office which adjoined the first aid room.

"Well, I don't know completely about his mission. I do know I have never met anyone as selfless. He seems as though he would sacrifice anything to save another human being."

"He would do that for sure. Did he tell you about his wife, Judith or his father-in-law?" Gary sat down in the solid oak chair on rollers behind a thick wood plank desk left over from the war department.

"No. I met his mother and one of his sons. We never talked about his wife." Bill Larkin sat in one of several oak arm chairs. The floor was wood as well as the floor-to-ceiling bookcases covering the two side walls. The wall with the windows facing the street was to Gary's back. The wall behind Bill had pictures of various VIPs who had visited the building over the years and the door to the medical facility.

"Paul Iscariot saved my daughter from a fatal accident on the freeway last Friday. I have so many questions to ask him. It is more important than I can express."

"I am sure it is, Mr. Larkin. But there are some things you must know about Paul Iscariot. Things that may have some influence regarding your desire to meet with him again."

Chapter 15
The Mission

"JUDITH ISCARIOT WAS IN El Salvador with her father in 1989. They had gone down there to see if Paul should go into the jungle and administer to the refugees suffering from the corrupt governments in Central America. While they were there, Judith was tortured and brutally murdered. It seems she and the guides helping them in their travel had stumbled onto a drug smuggling ring.

"The security guards thought it was a raid and killed everyone in the party, including Judith and her father. Paul got word and traveled to El Salvador in hopes of finding his wife and resurrecting her body. The bodies could not be found. It would have been too late even if he had found her and her father. There are certain principles even the Healer must abide by. The principles of God and nature."

"How did Paul react to the death of his wife?" Bill asked.

"He went in search of her murderers. They tried to kill him also but Paul and his fathers before him are well known in certain populations all over the world. A group of refugees smuggled his body back to the States. He was almost dead when they brought him here. We hid him and nursed him back to health. He has stayed here in Los Angeles to help the people so greatly in need.

"When he brought your daughter back to life, he exposed himself to the above ground world. A world that would not understand a man like Paul. A world that could possibly put an end to his great work. Do you want the responsibility of his end or the end of his family on your head, Mr. Larkin?"

"No, of course not. I don't want to see him stopped. I want to help him. I have witnessed the destruction of things we don't understand before. If a story as staggering as the one surrounding Paul Iscariot were to be brought to the public, it could change the world. There are people out there and I mean some very rich and powerful people that would give anything to have the Healer under their control."

"You are correct, Mr. Larkin. That is why you can't see Paul again. Exposure will mean an end to his mission."

Bill folded his hands and placed his elbows on the arms of the chair. "Gary, you keep talking about Paul's mission. Why don't you tell me what that mission is and how he plans to accomplish it." Bill was finally starting to see the need for Minister Gary Jenson to tell what it was that Paul Iscariot was here to accomplish. He had concluded, after his brief meeting with Paul, that every Paul Iscariot since 34 AD had been serving humanity. What greater mission could there be in life.

Gary started to speak. "Paul Iscariot is here to administer to mankind, that is true. He feels that the Los Angeles area, of all the geographical locations in the world, needs his services the most. But he is here because Los Angeles has the most to give back to the world."

Gary stood and walked toward the bookshelf. He withdrew a book from a tight fitting spot on one of the shelves. As he waked back to his chair, Bill could see that it was a Holy Bible.

"You see, Bill, ever since King James had the Bible translated into King's English and put the teachings of the prophets and apostles into one binding, man has tried to change it. Man has interpreted the Bible every which way till Sunday. Man has put his twist on the meaning of God's word and His relationship with man and so on and so on until no one, maybe not even God, knows what the original master plan was.

"Actually that is my own interpretation. I am sure God knows exactly what the original plan is. But it is like our constitution. It has been twisted and turned in so many directions to serve man it is almost rendered useless. The same way with the Bible. Whether you believe in the Christ child or not, Jesus had a mission on earth. It was to teach each and every one of us to love each other. To love is to respect one another's individuality but not let it get so out of hand that anyone's individuality becomes omnipotent.

"In the process of being an individual you must take on the responsibility of caring and watching out for the welfare of others. No matter the inconvenience, no matter the sacrifice you make of your own for another, the sacrifice must be made.

"It is actually quite simple. If you are a person that has a great deal and another has not, share what you have. A great deal to one person may be nothing to another and one person thinking he has little may seem to have it all, in the eyes of a person that has nothing. Paul has never had any great wealth, other than his spirit.

"What he has he gives, regardless of what the other person looks like, how they dress, their faith, or the color of their skin. It has been the commitment of every Iscariot since Judas. Greed has made it all so complicated. Paul is not in a position to eliminate greed or even overturn events allowing the greedy to prosper. He works with people one at a time."

Bill spoke up. "Then his mission is to be an example of how mankind must act in order to survive?" Bill stood and took the Bible from where Gary had laid it on his desk.

"I believe man will survive regardless of how successful Paul is with respect to his mission. It is the quality of life that will be affected if he fails. There is a passage in the Bible talking about how one can recognize a true believer. 'By his works, he shall be known.' The work referred to is that of human kindness."

"According to your interpretation. Don't get me wrong, I believe in the principles you are talking about. My main concern is for Paul and the only way I can help him is to see him. Do you know where I can find him?" Bill had looked at his watch and it was almost 11:30 a.m. Time was of the essence and he knew he had to find Paul soon or lose his opportunity to ever see him again.

"As I said before I do not know where to find Paul Iscariot. He could be anywhere."

"He is not here at the mission? Maybe you are hiding him like you did when the drug cartel was looking for him. I know you feel you are the best judge of what is good for Paul. I believe you would go to any length to protect him. It appears, from what you have said, millions of other people feel the same way. I honestly believe Paul should have the opportunity to decide for himself."

Bill took out a pen and notepad from his inside pocket. "Here is my cell phone number, my pager, direct line at work, and the number of my in-laws. Tell Paul I need to speak with him as soon as possible. Please ask him to call me. I can help him and I think you know I can."

Bill tore off the sheet of paper returning the pad and pen to his pocket and took out his wallet. He removed three hundred dollars from the inside fold and placed it in a collection plate on the corner of Gary's desk. "This isn't much but it will help you buy a few meals. I will be back, I promise. I would like to bring my family here to meet you and see the work you do. Would you allow us the privilege?" Bill was sincere.

"Yes, of course. We would be blessed to have you and your family participate in one of our special events. Thank you for the donation." Gary Jenson's attitude toward Bill changed dramatically.

Bill reached out to shake his hand and Gary placed the Bible he was holding into Bill Larkin's hands. Tears welled up in Bill's eyes. "I didn't grow up in a religious home; however, my parents were very kind people. They taught us to respect others and to 'Do unto others.' I believe the things you talked about this morning. We can all do more. I promise you, I mean no harm to come to Paul. Find him and have him call me. Please, Gary."

Bill turned and walked toward the office door. Gary Jenson walked next to him. "I will try my best to reach Paul Iscariot. If he wants to communicate with you the choice will be his. Thank you again for your generosity."

Bill Larkin walked down the steps and got into his car. It was noon and he had less than eighteen hours before he had to present his story to Stan Eversol. He drove to the 710 Freeway heading for his office. At twelve-fifteen his cell phone rang. He picked it up from the seat next to him and flipped open the mouthpiece.

"This is Bill Larkin."

"This is Paul Iscariot. I am sorry about the other night." Paul sounded different. Almost distant.

Bill spoke quickly. "I understand about the other night. Paul, I must see you. I know I can help you and your family. I can never repay you for returning my daughter's life to her mother and me. Where are you?" Bill pulled off at the next ramp figuring Paul must be close to the mission if Gary was able to reach him so quickly.

"I can't tell you where I am, Bill. However, I could meet you Thursday evening, before I leave." Paul's words came slowly.

"Can you tell me where you are going?" Bill returned to the freeway heading south toward Long Beach.

"No, I can't. You understand, don't you? It is the way the Iscariot family has survived for over 2,000 years. When there is too much exposure, we vanish into a new culture, a new city. We become part of the invisible inhabitants no one wants to see. Coincidentally the invisible are the people needing our help the most." Paul sounded stronger with each word.

"I do understand and I hope what you have done for my family is not the cause of your leaving." Bill knew Paul had to leave because of Adrian's miracle. But he had to keep Paul on the line long enough to get back to the mission.

"I involved myself understanding the consequences of my actions, Bill. I was hoping the outcome might be different. However, I also believe everything happens for a reason. It is time to move on. Surprisingly enough, it doesn't matter what city I reside in, the invisible people all have the same problems."

Doing his best thinking on his feet, Bill broke into Paul's comments. "Paul, excuse my interruption, I have an idea. What if you were to tell your story to me in front of a camera? I could air it only after you have left town. If we can capture the attention of the people of Los Angeles and it opens their eyes to your cause, furthering the effects of your mission, this could turn into an extremely positive situation. What do you think?" Bill waited. There was no response from Paul.

"Paul, are you still there?" There was still no answer. The exit leading to the Long Beach Mission Home was only one half-mile ahead. Bill continued to wait for Paul's response. "Paul, have I lost you? These God damned cell phones just when you need them the most—"

"I'm still here." Paul was in deep thought. "How much time do you need in order to be ready to interview me on camera?"

Bill felt encouraged by the response. "I can be ready at a moment's notice." Bill Larkin's excitement grew.

"Where would I meet you for the interview?" Paul was sounding positive. "Anywhere you like. I can have a remote unit on the street in less than five minutes. Shall I set it up right now?" Bill was anxious.

"We should really meet first and go over the information you want to cover prior to taping. Are you at the mission?" Bill sensed the story of the century and felt in his heart he could really help Paul accomplish his goal of teaching people how to

154

take an active part in helping others.

"Yes, I am at the mission."

"I knew it. Gary put up a good front. I knew you must be there somewhere."

"Gary?" Paul asked sincerely.

"Gary Jenson. I am almost back at the mission now. We can discuss the issues you want to cover most and prepare your presentation."

"I'm not at the Long Beach Mission. I am in Los Angeles, at the downtown facility. I will have to think about your proposal. It may be a great idea. I will get back to you."

The phone went dead. Bill tried to get Paul back on the phone but there was no response.

Chapter 16
Things Money Can't Buy

"MISS LEWIS, WOULD YOU please contact my physician and have him come to my office as soon as possible. I want him to look at my hand." Thomas released the intercom button and looked at his hand again. The swelling had increased in spite of the ice pack. The color continued to darken.

The masseuse had arrived on time and was standing naked next to the table preparing Thomas's favorite oils and lotions. Thomas showered and walked to the table, dropping his towel from his waist to the floor.

"Laurie, you look radiant today." Thomas took the liberty of kissing her hard on the mouth. She returned the kiss just as hard. She knew, as did all the women in Thomas's life, the way to Thomas B. Rich's wealth was in his pants. He paid them for sexual favors, for silence and for keeping clean. The women, each and every one, a former high-priced hooker, earned six figures a year being at the beck and call of the wealthiest man in the country.

They traveled with him during his various business trips. They attended dinner parties, public appearances, private meetings, looking more like women from the pages of *Playboy* than the prostitutes they were. Everyone knew and no one, not even Larry Dawkins, spoke to Thomas about his women. It was part of his public image. Part of the pride of wealth and Thomas Rich loved the attention.

"Give me a good hard rub, okay, baby? Just don't touch my right hand." Thomas held it up for her to see. Laurie winced at the sight of it. She didn't ask him how he had hurt it. Thomas's women spoke only when they were asked a question. They only answered questions asked by their boss. It was a standing rule. 'Speak only when spoken to and never to another man in the presence of Thomas Boy Rich.'

Doctor Smith arrived before the massage was completed. Miss Lewis announced his arrival over the intercom in the gym.

Thomas rolled onto his back and pointed to his cock. "Finish me off like a good girl, Laurie. I have a doctor's appointment." Laurie masturbated him to climax and left the room.

Thomas lay still for a few minutes and let the climax finish rippling through his body. He stood and walked toward the shower, stopping at the telephone hanging on the wall. "Miss Lewis, have the doctor meet me in my dressing room. Tell him I will join him as soon as I have showered. Offer him a drink." Thomas released the page button before Miss Lewis could answer.

"Doctor Smith, Mr. Rich would like you to join him in his dressing room. He will be out of the shower momentarily. Would you care for a drink?"

Dr. Levi Smith was a 45-year-old internal specialist from the UCLA Medical Center. When Thomas's previous doctor had retired, Thomas sent Larry on a quest to find the best of the best. He didn't want someone too old and detached from modern mainstream medicine, or one so young that Thomas could bully into telling him only what he wanted to hear. Dr. Levi Smith fit the requirements perfectly.

He had graduated form Harvard Medical School number one in his class. He was always looking for new methods to prevent illness rather than treat an illness as it came along. He had a pride in his own health even Thomas Rich admired. He was a wellness doctor and that is what Thomas demanded, to be well. In the ten years he had treated his foremost patient, Thomas Rich had only once been confined to bed because of a bug he had picked up while in Algeria two years earlier. Dr. Smith's prescription of diet, exercise and vitamin supplements had kept his patient in top shape as well as out of the hospital.

"Doctor Smith, thank you for coming on such short notice." Thomas extended his left hand to shake with Levi, holding up his right so the doctor could see it.

"Thomas, how did this happen?" Doctor Smith showed immediate concern.

"A freak accident. I hit it on the door handle in my office." The doctor continued to examine the hand pressing here and there, watching the reaction of his benefactor.

Thomas had gotten the appointment as head of new research and wellness medicine at UCLA for Levi Smith. He put the doctor in a position coveted by other doctors waiting for the opportunity to have funds and state-of-the-art equipment at their disposal. Dr. Smith became an instant icon in new medicine, and Thomas Rich had a doctor on call day or night, for the rest of his life.

"When did this happen, Thomas?" Dr. Smith's concern was apparent.

"This morning, just a few hours ago. Why? Does it look that bad? Ouch! Jesus, Levi, you squeezed the life out of my whole arm." Thomas pulled his hand back and shook it.

"Do you have any other symptoms or problems you have been neglecting?" Dr. Smith knew his patient well. Usually when Dr. Smith got a call from Thomas it was because he was run down or fighting off a cold. He wouldn't want to be bothered with seeing the doctor and being told to get some rest or take another vitamin. And Thomas Rich hated the sight of a needle.

"My neck and shoulders have been bothering me lately. I have been increasing the weight on my lifts and attributed the pain to sore muscles. Other than that and an occasional pestering cough, I can't think of anything."

The doctor took a digital body temperature instrument from his bag. He inserted it into Thomas's ear and almost instantly received a reading. "You have a low grade fever. Have you had any trouble sleeping or with eliminations?"

Levi took his blood pressure cuff and started to measure Thomas's blood pressure.

"Put that thing away. I have the best testing equipment in the world right here in the gym. My resting pulse is 72 and my blood pressure is 120 over 78. I bet that is better than yours on any given day."

"It may be better than mine but humor me and let me take your readings with these antiquated instruments they give us at the hospital."

Thomas sat quietly as the doctor squeezed the bulb.

"I show a slightly higher blood pressure than your reading, Thomas. You should have your equipment checked for accuracy." The doctor moved his fingers under Thomas's chin and around his neck, pressing in at various spots where the glands are located, and getting an immediate reaction of pain from his patient.

"I want to do a blood and urine sample on you as soon as I get back to the hospital. I'll draw the blood and you urinate in the cup." Ignoring Thomas's protest, Levi removed a syringe from his bag and filled the sterile plastic tube with dark burgundy blood. He put a patch on the insertion point and handed Thomas a plastic cup with a tight fitting lid. Thomas stood where he was and filled the container, handing it back to the doctor. Doctor Smith put his instruments in the bag and the blood and urine in a small chilled container he took from his bag.

"I'll have the results back by late afternoon. Will you be

here today or are you going out of town?"

Thomas looked at the doctor with a serious eye. "How does it look, Levi?"

"It's too soon to tell anything, Thomas. I will know better when the lab results come back. The hand does not look good, however. Keep ice on it and if you want something for the pain, I can give you a few painkillers."

"No, no. I don't believe in killing pain. It dulls the senses. Pain just heightens your awareness. Let me know as soon as you can. I will be in town until Friday."

Doctor Smith extended his hand for a shake but Thomas had turned and walked back toward the shower.

By late afternoon with the mall transaction complete and with everyone in the office already gone, Thomas and Larry Dawkins opened a bottle of Dom Perignon. Thomas raised his glass first.

"To my friend and fellow stockholder in Rich Fuels Incorporated, I toast our continued success."

The two men touched glasses and downed the sparkling wine. The phone in the outer office rang and Larry walked to Miss Lewis's desk to answer it.

"Yes, this is Mr. Dawkins. Hello, Doctor Smith. I wasn't aware you had been by today. Yes, he is standing in his office. One moment please, I will have him pick up." Larry pushed the hold button and walked back into the CEO's office.

"Thomas, it is Dr. Smith on line one. He would like to speak to you in private. I'll go clear my desk and wait for you in the lobby. Dinner reservations are for six. I'll have the driver come to the front of the building." Larry closed the double doors quietly and went to his office. He could tell there was something wrong by the sound of the doctor's voice.

When he finished, he returned to Thomas's office. He could tell Thomas was still inside so he knocked on the door. There was no answer. Larry opened the door slowly as he knocked again. Thomas was pale and had the look of death on his face.

"Thomas, what is it? What did the doctor say?" Larry hurried to Thomas's side. Thomas looked up at him from his chair. His eyes were suddenly red and swollen.

"Take me to the hospital, Larry. Levi wants to do some more tests." Thomas hung up the phone still resting in his hand.

"I will call the driver. He should already be waiting for us at the front door." Larry started to pick up the phone.

"I don't want a driver, you fool. Take me in your car. Do you think I want anyone to know I am going to the hospital? Dismiss the driver and cancel our evening."

Larry stood in silence and looked at Thomas.

"What are you waiting for—a funeral?" Thomas slammed his good fist into the desk, ignoring the pain.

Larry, realizing Thomas's pride would keep him from telling his only partner what the doctor said, drove in silence to the hospital. Parking the car in the emergency only space was at Thomas's insistence.

"Doctor Smith wants to take some more blood and do a scan with his new machine. If you want to go you can." It was the first time in Larry's memory that his friend and employer looked scared, of anything.

"Thomas, level with me. I have always taken a back seat to your decision making process. It has worked out better than I had ever imagined. Now you need someone you can confide in and I am that someone. Tell me what the doctor said on the phone. Please, Thomas." Larry Dawkins, leader of so many of the campaigns waged for the betterment of the T. B. Rich Corporation, realized his level of communication was rarely personal.

Thomas, except for the rare exception, never confided any personal truths to him. Larry considered how long they had known each other. In 1949 Thomas had come to school at Pepperdine University. He never talked about his parents, Samuel or Elizabeth Andersen. Larry realized the only history he had on Thomas B. Rich was the business dealings of the company and Thomas's appetite for money and women.

Larry saw Doctor Smith pass by an open door of the waiting room. "Doctor Smith." The doctor did not turn around.

"Doctor Smith, it's Larry Dawkins. Do you have a moment?"

Doctor Smith turned around and walked back to Larry. "I'm sorry, Mr. Dawkins. I was a million miles away from here. Actually my mind is 4,865 miles away. Mr. Dawkins, do you remember when Mr. Rich was sick around two and a half years ago?"

"Yes, I do. It was right after he returned from Algeria upon the conclusion of negotiations for pipeline rights. Algeria was the last country to sign on in the area of the Mediterranean Sea. Why do you ask?"

"There is a possibility that a latent virus has been working overtime in Mr. Rich's system. It is all but undetectable under even the most rigorous of physical exams. It usually goes undetected until death."

Larry turned white and sweat started dripping down his forehead. "Are you telling me Mr. Rich is dead?"

"No. But he is dying. I am sorry, Mr. Dawkins. I know how close the two of you are."

Larry closed his eyes and turned toward the wall.

"Mr. Rich has an extremely rare virus called Allatoxin Veritus. It attacks the largest single organ of the body; the skin. As it spreads, it replaces healthy oxygen bearing cells with diseased cells. Once it has taken over the majority of healthy cells say, in the hand, and the area infected is injured in any way, it releases a toxin produced by the diseased cells. Those cells quickly capture cells with a healthy oxygen supply and consume them. When an area of the body is injured, it starts a chain reaction. Slowly at first but gaining momentum as the exposure to healthy cells increases. Once the area is consumed by the virus, it turns black from lack of oxygen. Death can occur in less than 96 hours."

Larry was stunned. He leaned back against a wall and covered his face with his hands.

"How long does he have?" Larry removed a handkerchief from his coat pocket and wiped his tears.

"Less than two days. I haven't told him yet. I was going to talk to you once I received completed confirmation from the disease control center in Atlanta. He gave me explicit instructions not to tell anyone, regardless of his condition, until I talked to him. I think you should be there when I tell him." The doctor took Larry's arm and helped him stand away from the wall.

"I don't know what to say. Can't you remove his hand or arm and stop this from spreading?" Larry was frantic.

"No, not at this stage. It moves so fast it cannot be stopped with amputation. Does he have any relatives living?"

Larry looked toward the ceiling and made fists of both hands. "Not that I know of. His parents died when we were in college. I am sure he was an only child. There were no other family members at the funeral."

Chapter 17
The Message

BILL LARKIN SPENT THE day organizing a plan for the meeting with Paul. He was working on his list of questions that would bring Paul Iscariot into public view just enough to get his message across without exposing him to the point of losing his ability to carry out his work. It caused Bill to sit back in his chair and wonder to himself.

"What kind of sacrifice has this person made to spend his entire life devoted to the service of others? When does he take care of himself? He really doesn't see himself as number one. How does he finance his work? If he could give the world one message what would it be?" Bill leaned forward and put his elbows on his desk. He rubbed his eyes and looked at his watch. It was 4:55 p.m. He was concerned about what time Paul Iscariot would call, or if he would call. His phone rang.

"Hello, this is Bill. No, Jane, I haven't heard anything from our Mystery Man." Bill leaned forward in his chair and started tapping a pencil on his desk.

"Do you want me to let the crew go for the evening?" Jane wanted to leave but did not want to miss out on being part of the Mystery Man's interview.

"No, let's keep the crew intact. I don't know when or if our call will come today.

"They are starting to growl for food and drinks." Jane was always on top of her staff's needs. She treated them like a mother hen.

"Call the deli and place an order for whatever they want." Bill wasn't too hungry at the moment. His thoughts had been too ingrained regarding Paul to think about food.

"Do you mind if I go? I have a date this evening, but I will stay as late as you like. My plans can be canceled with no problem."

Jane was going to meet Larry and confirm plans for their trip to Greece. Bill made it a point to keep a distance from the personal lives of his staff. He knew Jane had a boyfriend but never asked about him. Whenever there was a social function, Jane went with Bill if Susan was unable to go. If Susan was to attend with Bill, Jane would bring one of the male members of the staff.

"You deserve some free time. Between covering for me and keeping up with the museum opening, you must be exhausted. By the way, thanks." Bill was sincere. He truly appreciated Jane's hard work and her reliability.

"Would you do one more favor for me before you leave? Make sure the pagers and cell phone batteries are 100% so I can reach any one of the crew when I need them. And bring me a current list of phone and pager numbers so I can have it with me." Bill wrote several notes as he paused.

"Yes, is there anything else I can get you before I leave? Do you want me to order something for you to eat?" Jane was looking for a newly sharpened pencil.

"I'm surprised you asked, you usually order food for me out of reflex." Bill smiled to himself and rubbed his stomach.

Jane laughed out loud on the other end of the phone. "I would hate for you to go hungry. I thought you might be going home to see Susan and the kids. That's why I asked." Jane admired the Larkins. If she were ever to have a family, she wanted to be as good a parent as Bill or Susan. Always involved with their children and sharing their interests. Unlike the family she had grown up with.

"No. I'm not going home just yet. I want to be here if our man calls. Thank you anyway, Jane." Bill hung up the phone and turned in his chair. He looked out over the city and wondered where Paul was at this moment.

"Maybe he's left town already. I know I can help you," Bill thought out loud as he leaned back putting his hands behind his head and closing his eyes.

The door swung open as Jane Turner entered in a rush and dropped the phone list on Bill's desk. Bill opened his eyes and turned his chair slowly seeing only Jane's back as she headed for the door.

"Is this all of the numbers I will need? What about home numbers if I let the crew go before the call?"

Without turning back Jane answered, increasing her volume as she got further away. "That's all you'll need. If you send anyone home, they will call me and let me know where they are and how I can reach them in case their pager doesn't work. If you need any or all of the gang, call me, my numbers are the first two on the list. I'll call everyone else. See you in the trenches." She waived over her head as she continued down the hall.

"Thank you for your efficiency, Jane. I'll remember you next Christmas." Bill turned his chair back toward the window. The moment he dozed off, the phone rang.

Bill answered, "Hello, this is Bill. Susan, I was just going to call you. No, I haven't heard from Paul. I have been holding the mobile unit and crew hostage all day. No, I haven't eaten lunch or dinner. I think it is best if I stay here and wait for Paul's telephone call. What time is it?" Bill looked at his watch. It was 6:20 p.m.

"Bill, Elaine and I are going to take the boys to the mall and do some shopping. If all goes well, I am going to take them to school tomorrow and ease them back into our regular routine.

I drove by the school this afternoon and there were no reporters. I called the school office and they said no one has called."

"What about Adrian?" Bill held the picture of the kids in his left hand. The one they had given him last Father's Day.

"Adrian is fine, but I don't feel comfortable leaving her at school yet. The principal said he would have a work package for her tomorrow when I drop off the boys. She can do her homework here and at home if we go home this weekend. Do you think we can go home this weekend?" Susan was missing home and anxious to get back to normal.

"I don't see why not. There won't be any reason to stay away if I don't hear from Paul Iscariot."

"What do you mean?" Susan asked.

"If we don't hear from Paul by tomorrow, he has left the city. Probably for another country. Maybe Mexico, or Peru, I don't know." Bill was getting more tired by the moment.

"What does Mr. Iscariot's staying or going have to do with us going home?"

"Once his story hits the mainstream, there will be press members of every size and shape from all over the world here in Los Angeles trying to find him. They will leave no stone unturned. They will find Adrian, the school, my office, our home everything. What will we do then?"

"We'll deal with it, sweetheart, one day at a time. It will pass. It always does." Susan's voice was calm and direct.

"I don't know, Susan. There are so many crazies in the world today. Who knows what might happen? I am not even sure I want the story at this point." Bill was tired.

"You said you felt there was something good you could do for Paul. I think we owe him anything we have to offer."

"He doesn't want anything. I'm the one pushing the interview and in the interview the story of Adrian and the accident will be brought out. I feel it is an extremely important part of his message. Faith healed a little girl and people need to know why Paul Iscariot's faith is so strong." Bill was coming back to life; his reporter mind working fast.

"Why is Paul Iscariot's faith so strong?" Susan had been asking the same question in her prayers.

"I don't know, baby. I really don't know. But it is a question that keeps coming back into my mind over and over as I write down what to ask him, if the interview happens. What do you think I should ask him?" Bill was serious.

"Ask him what the people watching the report can do for one another. Ask him how they can help spread his message." Susan smiled and Bill felt her warmth even though he could not see her.

"You never cease to amaze me, Susan. You are so practical, so intuitively smart. It's just that simple. Ask him in front of 100 million viewers, what his message is and how we can help him. If that be the case then Adrian must be present. He will need her for credibility. What do you think?" Bill paused.

"I worry about how it will affect her life. She will be an instant international celebrity. Can she live with that?" Susan had a trace of fear in her voice.

"You know what I could do? The crew is here and the equipment is all set for a remote, I'll bring them to the house and interview you and Adrian then replay the tape prior to the interview with Paul." Bill was wide-awake by now. "Susan, hold for a minute, OK?"

Without waiting for a response Bill put her on hold and pushed the intercom button for the cafeteria. "Hey, boys and girl, are you there?"

Patricia answered, "Just me. I'm setting everything up for eats. Are you going to join us?"

"No. In fact, plans have changed. Cancel the food. I'm taking you guys to dinner."

Bill pushed the hold button and cut off Patricia's response.

"Susan, I'm sorry. What do you think? Do you think you and Adrian are up for that kind of a situation? I could keep both of your faces in a shadow and use generic names, you know to protect the innocent. Your taped interview along with Paul's live interview would convince anyone of Paul's sincerity and his faith." Bill was writing notes as he spoke.

"I don't know, Bill. How long would it take before some eager reporter or an informant told the world that the mother and daughter in the miracle on I-5 were you wife and daughter? Then, what would happen? You have been right to keep Adrian away from the press for all of the reasons you've stated."

"I know. It's just that I want to give something back to Paul Iscariot for the sacrifice he made for us. I want it to be—well you know, the best we have to give."

"I know, Bill, and we will. You will think of the best way to help Paul. If you feel that includes an interview with Adrian and me so be it. I support your decision."

"Susan, with clips of the sky cam tape made on the day of the accident and both of your interviews on tape it will make Paul Iscariot's message undeniable. It will give him the credibility he needs to be believed."

"Maybe he isn't worried about how his message is received!" Susan added.

"I know. I think he truly feels that way. My contribution to his success is the presentation of his message so it will be believed. There will be those who won't believe anything Paul says. But if one person believes and acts on that belief for the benefit of another human being, his message will be a success. That is what I want to give him." Bill sat back and let out a long breath.

"Bill Larkin, I love you." Susan started to cry softly.

"Sweetheart, it's the least I can do. What time are you going to be back from the mall?"

"What time do you want me back?"

"The crew is here and ready to go. I'll finish up, take them to dinner and be at your dad's house by 8:00. We will take about ten of fifteen minutes to set up and I can interview

Adrian first. Can you be back by 8:30?" Bill was looking at his watch. Susan did the same.

"Yes. I'll have the boys and Elaine with me. When we get back to the house, I will explain what is going on before we come in. That should cut down a little of the excitement and confusion."

"Thank you, Susan. I'll see you at 8:30. Oh, by the way, I love you too." Bill hung up the phone and went back to his notes. He pushed the intercom button on his desk and alerted the waiting crew.

"Get ready to saddle up, boys and girl. We're going to Jerry's and then for an interview in Bel Air in one hour. It's showtime." Bill took his finger off the button and the voices of the crew came back as a cheer.

"Is it time to meet the Miracle Man?" asked Wes.

"No, we are going to interview the little girl." Bill's voice came back on the intercom. The crew stood and looked at each other for a long moment.

"How did he find the little girl?" asked Mark.

"Don't ask, just do!" responded Patricia.

"Janie said he knew the family," Max added.

"Let's get ready, newshounds, time's a wasting." Wes shut off the lights.

Chapter 18
Death Sentence

"THOMAS, I ASKED MR. DAWKINS to join us. I know you told me otherwise; however, as your doctor, I felt you should have your closest friend with you." Levi closed the hospital door behind him.

"Cut the bullshit, Levi, and let me have it." Thomas was putting his shirt on over an ice pack taped to his injured hand.

"Thomas, you are going to die, and I can't do a damn thing about it. Is that straight enough for you?" Dr. Smith crossed his hands around his clip chart and leaned against the door.

"It's plain enough but I don't believe it. What do you mean you can't do anything about it? I've spent millions of dollars helping you make this one of the most advanced medical centers in the world. Now you think you can stand there and tell me you can't do anything? That's absurd." Thomas continued to dress.

"Thomas, the doctor's right. You have a rare disease called—what is it, Doc?"

"Allatoxin Veritus."

Doctor Smith moved away from the door and toward Thomas. "It's true, Thomas. It is something you picked up in Algeria a few years ago and—"

Larry was cut short by Thomas. "Bullshit on you too,

Dawkins. You don't know what in the fuck you're talking about and I'm not going to stand here and listen to either of you." Thomas grabbed his suit coat and walked to the door.

"Thomas, for God's sake stop and listen to us."

Thomas Rich pushed open the door with his swollen hand and stopped short in pain.

Larry ran to him. "Thomas, you have less than 48 hours to live."

Thomas was bent over in pain. His back was turned toward Larry. As he turned, Larry and Dr. Smith could see a deep reddish purple flush come over him. The pain causing a demonic expression on his face.

"God damn it, my hand. Get me the best doctors money can buy. I'll spend anything—everything—to be well. Don't stand there and tell me it can't be done."

"Thomas, have I ever lied to you? If anything can be done it will be. This disease is almost an unknown and all reported cases to date have been fatal. I have staff working overtime contacting every medical center on the planet via computer. We will try anything coming back that gives us hope. I need you to stay in the hospital so we can act immediately on any information as we get it." Levy put his hand on Thomas's shoulder.

"I'll come back when you are ready to cure me. Until then I will return to my office with Mr. Dawkins. Call me there. Mr. Dawkins, we're leaving." Thomas turned and forced his shoulder into the door.

Larry and Dr. Smith looked at each other and shrugged their shoulders. "I won't leave his side, Doctor. Call me as soon as you have anything." Larry followed Thomas down the hall.

Thomas stopped and turned, pointing at Dr. Smith over Larry's shoulder. "Not a word of this to anyone, Levi, understand?"

Levi Smith nodded and waved his hand. Then spoke only to himself. "Don't worry, Mr. Rich. You'll be dead before it could ever be on the weekend news."

Thomas and Larry went back to the office. The ride there was silent. Larry Dawkins parked the car in front of the building in a reserved parking space. Before he could turn off the engine, Thomas was out of the car and through the front doors of Rich Plaza.

Larry followed Thomas up to the top floor of the complex in another elevator. He stopped long enough at the reception desk, using the phone to call in an order for food and drinks. He knew they would not leave the office before dawn. He walked into Thomas's office and went to the desk next to the wall.

"Would you like a drink, Thomas?" Larry poured himself a large glass of private label brandy.

"The usual and make it double." Thomas was already taking papers out of his safe and arranging them on his desk.

"If word of this leaks out, our stock will drop at the morning bell on Wall Street."

"It won't leak out, Thomas." Larry handed him his drink and took a swallow of his own.

"Besides, by morning Doctor Smith may have found something that can help you!"

"Drop it, Dawkins. There is nothing he can do unless his diagnosis is wrong. And I doubt he is wrong or he would not have said anything. When did he tell you I had 48 hours?" Thomas was sitting behind his desk. He reached for his brandy and took a long slow drink until the glass was empty.

"In the hall before we came into your room. He thought it would be better if I knew and was there when he told you." Larry sat in a chair in front of Thomas's desk. "Is there anyone you want me to call, anyone you would like to see between now and—"

Thomas cut him off. "Before I'm fucking dead? Is that what you were going to say?" Thomas stood and threw his empty glass across the office shattering it on the entry doors.

Larry stood and walked to the doors, turning to look at Thomas. He was leaning over his desk with his hands spread apart, both fists clenched, both fists black from lack of oxygen bearing cells.

"Where are you going?" Thomas asked without looking up.

"To my office. I'll be back in a minute." Larry walked through the double doors closing them behind him. He stood for a moment with his back pressed hard against the wood doors. Tears were in his eyes. The man that had made him rich, the man leading him since college, his best friend, was rotting away before his very eyes.

Larry Dawkins went to his office and sat in the dark. As he finished his drink, he turned on the desk lamp using the gold chain hanging down from under the green glass covering the bulb. He removed a personal phone directory and pulled the tab marked T. Under the name Turner he searched for the cell phone number of his longtime lover.

He remembered how Jane Turner had been one of Thomas B. Rich's girls in the late eighties. The most beautiful girl Larry had ever seen. After working for Thomas for five years, Jane became pregnant. Keeping from getting pregnant was the girls' direct responsibility according to Thomas. He insisted on an abortion and once he was sure there would be no child with his name on it, he threw Jane out.

When she arrived at her apartment after leaving the clinic, she had been evicted. Her clothes, furnishings—everything. When she went back to her car it was gone. Thomas did not allow this kind of carelessness and used Jane as an example for the other girls.

Larry recalled how devastated Jane was. She talked about suicide. When she finally called him, she was drunk and taking pills. He went to her and he fell in love. Using some of his own contacts, Larry got her a job with KBLA news working in the field of business reporting. With inside information from Larry Dawkins she created a powerful image as an insider breaking many stories as exclusives.

He often regretted the fact they had never married or moved in together. Vacations to exotic islands or a weekend getaway to out-of-the-way places were all they were free to share. He knew, even after all of the years of friendship and service he had given Thomas, if Thomas ever found out about Jane and him, he would be evicted also. Larry called her cell phone number and waited five rings before she answered.

"Hello, this is Jane." Jane was talking loud over some kind of background music.

"Janie, Larry. Where are you?" Usually when he called she would be at the studio, home or at the Press Club.

"I'm at the Press Club, where are you?" She moved toward the ladies' room so she could hear better.

"I'm at the office. Listen, something serious has come up. I need your help. Get to a private spot as soon as possible, then page me. I will call you back immediately."

"Are you all right?" She could tell by the sound of his voice it was serious.

"Yes, I'm fine. Just call me as soon as you can." Larry hung up the phone.

Jane stood in the restroom and stared at her cell phone. She looked in the mirror, fixing her makeup and hair. Jane walked back to the table and retrieved her jacket, excusing herself by saying she had to return to the office.

The KBLA studio was only two blocks away from the Press Club. The club had been established in the 1920s after the stock crash and had a reputation as the main hangout spot for people in the know regarding business.

Jane paged Larry as soon as she sat down at her desk. A few minutes later her phone rang.

"This is Jane." She removed the earring from her right ear and pressed the phone closer.

"Janie, is your phone secure?" Larry was obviously nervous.

"I think so. No one monitors phones at news stations

anymore. It violates too many freedom of the press issues. Why, Larry, what's the matter?" Jane showed concern in her voice.

"Thomas Rich is dying." There was complete silence on the phone.

"Is he in the hospital? Was it an accident? How long does he have to live?" Jane was writing notes like any good reporter would. Her mind was racing. How would it affect her special on the museum?

"He is here at the office. He has a rare virus and less than 48 hours to live. I need your help. I need to contact the man that healed the little girl on the freeway. Can you reach him?"

"No, not yet. My boss is waiting for him to call so we can do an exclusive interview. He has no known address or phone in the city. What are you thinking?"

"What do you think! I want him to come and heal Thomas. At this point I am willing to try anything." Larry knew Thomas would not stand for such a ridiculous idea. So did Jane.

"Do you think Thomas would go along with this idea?" Jane asked anyway. She was thinking of the story it would make: 'Richest man in America, healed at death's door.' She would be world famous for a story with that kind of impact.

"No, not at the moment. If I bring in the Healer and Thomas could see his powers, maybe I can convince him to try it as a last resort. He has no choice." Larry sat back in his chair.

"The minute I hear where he is, I will call you. The last report I received from one of my crew members, they were going to interview the little girl who was healed."

"Who is the little girl?" Larry sat straight up and reached for a pen.

"It's my boss's daughter."

"You mean the little girl is Bill Larkin's kid?"

"Yes."

"Where is she? What is the address?" Larry was sounding desperate.

"I don't have the address. She and her family are staying with Susan Larkin's parents."

"Can you get the address for me?" Larry stood up and paced the length of the phone receiver cord.

"Yes, Larry. What are you going to do?" Jane felt a twinge of fear in her heart.

"I don't know. But time is short. Very short, and I will have to act quick. Just get me the address and keep me informed if the Healer calls." Larry hung up without saying good-bye.

Jane knew about some of his business dealings and knew he was capable of going to any extreme to achieve his goals. He was a Thomas Rich protégé from the word go.

As Larry hung up his phone, he looked up from his desk. Thomas was standing in the shadow behind the desk lamp.

Chapter 19
The Interview

BILL LARKIN HAD THE mobile crew follow him to Westwood Village. Jerry's Famous Deli was open 24 hours a day, 7 days a week and offered a menu even Donald Trump could pick from. It was also one of the KBLA staff hangouts and the hostess found a large table for all of them so they could sit together. The food was served hot, the drinks ice cold. Bill was hungry. Figuring it to be a long night, he ordered plenty to eat. Two bites into dinner, his cell phone rang.

"This is Bill." There was no response from the other end.

"Hello, this is Bill Larkin. Hello?" Bill could hear voices in the background as though the caller on the other end was partially covering the mouthpiece.

"Bill, Bill Larkin?" the voice asked.

"Yes, this is Larkin. Who's asking?" Bill strained his ear to hear over the noise and cell phone static.

"Paul Iscariot. Do you still want to meet?" Paul put his hand over the phone again.

Bill took out a pad of paper and pen. "Yes. Where and when?" Bill motioned to the crew to wrap up their meals.

"Now, at the downtown Rescue Mission. Come to the back and knock on the steel door in the alley at the rear of the building. How long will it take you to get here?"

"We're in Westwood. I'd say 20 to 30 minutes depending on traffic. Will you wait?" Bill wrote 'LA Rescue Mis 30 min.' as he was getting to his feet and motioning the crew toward the door.

"Yes, I'll wait. I need to talk to you. How many of you are there?"

"Five. A news crew with a van and myself. I'll do the interview." Bill's heart was beating like it did in the old days when he was hot on the trail of a big scoop.

"Can you trust them?" Paul sounded concerned.

"How do you mean, Paul?" Bill did not want to lose him.

"Can you trust them to keep our meeting place secret?"

"I think so, why?" Bill was thinking ahead to see if he felt any doubts about the crew members.

"I feel something. Like a dark cloud approaching. It has me concerned. Maybe I'm just getting paranoid in my old age." Paul laughed an uneasy laugh.

Bill was constantly amazed how normal a man Paul seemed to be on the outside. The thought gave him an additional angle on the story.

"Do you want me to come alone?" Bill did not want to, but he offered.

"Would you?" Paul sounded relieved.

"Yes, if you want me to. Paul, I want to help your cause by producing a professional presentation of your message. I think big, you must think protection. Tell me what you want and you will have it."

"The fewer the number of people the better. I don't want to take any chances with my mother and son. Can you understand?" Paul sounded more relieved with each word.

"Yes, I fully understand. I feel the same way about Adrian and Susan being exposed to who knows what kind of danger. I'll come alone. I'll be there in thirty minutes. Thank you, Paul." Bill closed the cell phone and it shut off automatically. He paid the check and met the crew at the van.

"Bad news, boys and girl, the man wants to see me alone. I wish I could take you with me. This man is one of a kind. He's afraid of being compromised. He has a lot to lose and after what he has done for me. I must respect his request." Bill looked through the van for the equipment necessary to handle the remote alone.

"What did he do for you, boss?" Max asked.

"Is this guy on the level?" Mark chimed in.

Bill turned slowly, feeling he owed the crew some explanation for the hours they had waited. "The little girl in the accident was my daughter."

The crew was dumbstruck.

"I don't want that repeated to anyone, is that understood?" Everyone nodded their heads.

"Then the guy is on the level. He's a real miracle worker." Patricia smiled.

"What can we get you for the shoot?" Wes added.

"Set me up with a tripod, a camera, extra batteries, extra film and an audio system I can plug directly into the video camera. I want to get the best sound possible. This may be my only shot. I'll open the trunk of my car. Mark, if you and Patricia would pick out the equipment I need and, Max, if you would please run it through a quick checkout, I would appreciate it. And thanks guys for being so understanding." Bill was sincere.

"That's OK, boss. Just go and get a Pulitzer of your very own." Everyone laughed but Mark.

"I promise you will be in on the editing of the final tape. How's that? If there is any credit to be taken, we share it equally. Deal?" Bill held out his right hand.

Each member of the crew put their right hand on Bill's. Everyone repeated, "Deal!" except Mark.

Bill Larkin, his car loaded with enough equipment to tape a space shuttle landing, headed for the Mission District in downtown Los Angeles. *The area around the old Mission can*

180

be hazardous to say the least, he thought. In the daytime the homeless gathered openly on the streets surrounding the area. Urinating, puking, defecating at will, most of the transients having lost all respect for themselves and the rest of mankind. These were the ones that often could not even meet the minimal requirements to enter the Rescue Mission on a regular basis. The jails were too crowded and other crimes were of a higher priority than some man exposing himself during elimination to a group of secretaries walking from a parking lot to their office building. At night it was even worse. Drug abuse, alcohol and sex between consenting and non-consenting adults went unchecked.

When Bill Larkin's gold tinted Lexus turned into the alley he was pleased to recognize a familiar face. Dennis Chapman the police officer he met at the Junkyard was standing at the steel door. He motioned Bill to park against the building and opened his car door.

"Good evening, Officer Chapman." Bill shook his hand. "I didn't expect a police escort at this time of night."

"Paul asked me to stay with him for the evening and I told him I would take a couple of vacation days and stay with him until he leaves town. He's nervous. I have never seen him this way. Also I figure I owe him. What can I help you with?"

"If you wouldn't mind helping me with some of the equipment in the trunk." Bill opened the trunk. "Is there anyone else inside that can carry some equipment?"

"Yeah, I'll get a couple of the mission staff to pitch in. Hold the door open for me and I'll come right back."

Chapman grabbed the battery packs and put the tripod over one shoulder. Bill was happy to see him. Being in the Junkyard with Paul had not given him any cause to feel in danger. Downtown at night did.

Three men came back with Officer Chapman and helped Bill with the gear from his trunk. One of them stayed with the car. Once inside the building, they walked through a series of halls and up two flights of stairs. Paul was sitting in an average-sized room with a desk, a cot, and dim lighting except for the desk lamp.

"Bill, good to see you. Thank you for coming alone. Can you set up your equipment in here?" Paul helped with the tripod and battery cables.

"This room will be fine. I will need some more lighting if possible. Two or three floor lights will be a great help."

"I'll go round some up from the dorm," said Dennis Chapman.

"Thank you, Dennis." Paul followed him to the door.

"I'm sorry about the police protection but I don't know what else to do. I need to finish some business in the city and leave as soon as possible. How is Adrian?"

"She is well. I think after you have gone and I air the tape, life will back to normal." Bill continued making connections and testing the audio equipment.

"Bill, what is normal for you?" Paul sat in his chair and folded his arms in front of him.

"You know—school, homework, soccer, the job etc. etc. The usual stuff."

"I feel it only fair to warn you, your life will never return to that state of normality."

"What do you mean? Why should it be any different?" Bill stopped what he was doing and looked intently at Paul.

"Your family has been touched directly by God."

Bill looked like he was in shock. "How do you mean that? Are you telling me you are God?" Bill walked close to Paul.

Paul stood and reached out to take Bill's arm. "No, I am not God. But God chose the circumstances we find ourselves in and the outcome is yet to be determined." Paul spoke softly.

"How do you know this? What has yet to be determined?" Bill's face was sweating and the sweat streamed into his eyes.

"I don't know for sure, Bill. Only the next 24 hours will tell. I have had enough dealings with the power of God and his influence on man to know something is yet to happen." Paul let go of Bill's arm and walked toward the door.

"How long will the interview take?" Paul turned back to Bill.

"That depends on your message. Do you know what you want to say?" Bill went back to work on the video camera. "Would you like to be standing or sitting when you are speaking?"

"I don't know. What do you think would be better?" Paul sat back down in the chair.

"Lighting is going to be a problem. I'm not sure standing will give us a good light on your face. With floor lights and the one direct camera light I have we can probably get our best shot of you from the chair you are sitting in. Turn it away from the desk and angle it toward the camera." Bill bent to look through the lens.

"Like this?" Paul crossed one leg and folded his arms on his lap.

"Yes, that's it. If we put one or two floor lamps on the desk giving the background some light and one on the floor next to you, I think it will work."

Dennis Chapman came back into the room with another man. Both were carrying a lamp in each hand.

"Will these work?" asked Dennis.

"Plug them in for me and put two of them on the desk on the outside corners." Bill continued looking through the lens.

"Move the lamp on the right closer to Paul's left shoulder. Good. Now tilt the shade just a little and direct the light on his back. Great. How does that feel, Paul?"

"Fine, I guess. You're the professional."

Bill hooked up the audio and extended a microphone just off camera pointed at Paul's mouth. "Give that a check by speaking normally. About anything, just act like it isn't there." Bill made a few adjustments with the level transmitters and knobs.

"Though I walk through the valley of the shadow of death…" Paul stopped when Chapman burst into the room.

"Six men just came in the front door asking for Bill Larkin. They look like FBI but they're not. That means they're high-priced gunmen. I give you even odds they are carrying some serious weapons. I checked the back. The way is clear to your car, Bill. You take Paul and get the hell out of here. Paul, I'll catch up to you at our usual rendezvous. You and Bill stay together and wait for me. If I'm not there in an hour, leave town just the way we planned. If I don't make it look for contact from Reilly or Wilson. Got it?" Both men nodded. "Then get the hell out of here!"

Bill grabbed his camera and the battery pack. Paul took a small suitcase and a duffel bag. The sound of gunshots came from somewhere within the building. Bill put Paul in front of him in case someone came up from behind and tried to stop them. The way to the car was clear and two men from the mission were standing in the alley waiting for them. They both had baseball bats. Both men were large and looked like they could do as much damage with a bat as most men could with a gun.

More shots rang out and people inside the mission started to scream. Bill drove down the alley and out toward the Harbor Freeway. Paul put his hand on Bill's arm.

"Bill, we must go back. I may be able to help someone at the mission."

"You heard what Chapman said. You're in danger. Those men came looking for you. And who knows what may have happened to you. It could have been the end of your work."

"They may have been after me, but they asked for you."

Bill looked over at Paul and realized for the first time what that meant. "One of my own people. You asked for me to meet you alone. What else does your spirit guide tell you, Paul?"

"My mission is close to an end."

Chapter 20
The First Shall Be Last

BILL AND PAUL WENT to the Junkyard and parked on the deserted road where the bus had been used to make the pickup the night of the sweep. It was 11:15 p.m. There was a low fog rolling in and it made their car invisible to all except someone that might walk into it.

"Paul, would you like to use the phone?" Bill held out his cell phone.

"No, my mother and son are with Manny. They are leaving by plane tomorrow. I will join them as soon as possible, depending on what happens here over the next few hours."

Bill turned on the dome light. "What could happen? Are you expecting something you haven't told me about?"

"No. Just wondering out loud."

"I need to call Susan and tell her what happened. I don't want her to worry. I called her before I saw you and left a message with my father-in-law." Bill flipped open his phone and the battery was dead. He opened the trunk and looked for another one but realized he had left his spares at the mission.

"Damn it," Bill barked.

"Are you OK, Bill?" Paul was standing next to him looking into the trunk.

"Yeah, everything's fine. I left the batteries for the phone at the mission and the power cord for the cigarette lighter is broken. It's all right. I'll call Susan as soon as Chapman gets here. Do you have any batteries in your duffel bag? You've carried that thing everywhere since you left your house, haven't you? What's in there?"

"Susan won't be worried about you, Bill. She knows you are in good company."

Bill closed the trunk and both men got back into the car. There was a long silence.

"I don't have any batteries. And the answer to your second question is the physical proof." Paul sat back and closed his eyes.

"The physical proof of what?" Bill looked at the bag resting on the floor between Paul's feet. Paul did not respond. Bill could tell he was in deep thought.

"Bill, what is your religious background?"

Paul looked at him straight-faced. "My family was Protestant. I was never really involved. We went to church on special occasions—Christmas, Easter, weddings, and funerals. Mostly for my grandmother's sake. That's pretty much it."

Bill thought back to his own wedding. "Susan was raised Catholic. Her mom had a lot of problems and died when she was young. Her aunt and uncle raised her in their religion. We were married in a Catholic church with a full Catholic ceremony. More out of respect for her aunt and uncle than for us. Why do you ask?" Bill turned in his seat so he could look at Paul's face.

"I was wondering what kind of exposure you had as a child to the gospels, if any. How much do you know about the Bible?" Paul reached into his right shirt pocket and took out a stick of gum.

"Not much. Susan started reading her dad's after the accident. That's the first time I have seen a Bible since, I can't remember. Pretty weak excuse, isn't it?" Bill felt ashamed.

"No, not really. Most people fall into that category. At least the people living in Los Angeles. There are so many other things to be involved in. The poorer countries of the world—the ones without television, CDs and computers have little else to do except read the Bible. There are many eternal truths contained in those pages. And the Bible isn't the only book written by men of God."

"Considering what is involved in our daily lives in this day and age, isn't the Bible just a tad outdated?" Bill was serious.

"If you took everything out of the Bible except the Ten Commandments, those ten lines alone would keep today's man constantly busy trying to live by those principals. Wouldn't you agree?" Paul offered Bill a stick of gum.

"If man lived by the commandments, it would be a different world, that's for damn sure." Bill apologized for using the word damn.

"No matter. At least you didn't use the name of God in vain. Do you ever pray?" Paul was very serious.

"Sure, sometimes. I prayed for Adrian, Susan and the boys as soon as I heard about the accident. I was so relieved when I got to the hospital to find them alive and well I can't tell you."

"You don't have to tell me. I know what you felt. Have you ever prayed for anyone other than a family member?" Paul cracked the window and let in some air.

"I prayed for the Kennedys when the President and his brother were shot. I prayed for the King family when Martin Luther was shot also. It would be a better world if everyone lived by the commandments, wouldn't it?" Bill was almost whispering.

"I can't argue with that, Bill Larkin. If just half of the human race lived by the commandments it would be a world unlike any you have ever dreamed of. If half of the people on earth lived good lives and sacrificed to help the other half, it wouldn't be long before the world would be like heaven. For now, I am happy to find one out of many who live by a divine code."

Paul opened the car door and stepped out into the night air. "Did you hear something?"

Bill got out of the car also. "No. I just wanted to listen to the fog horn at the harbor entrance. I am going to miss Los Angeles. I think some good can be done in this city." Paul listened.

"I know, Paul, that's why I wanted to record your message." Bill sat on the hood of his car and pulled his jacket tight around his neck.

"You have my message, Bill. You know it by heart. You know what you have to do in order to share it with the people of Southern California. After tomorrow it will be your responsibility. But like anything else, it will be up to you. The path you take, your dedication to spreading the word and spirit of the message."

Bill cut him off. "Wait a minute. I'm not going to turn into a preacher, Paul. I told you I would do anything for you, Susan and I have made that commitment. The best thing I can do is broadcast your message, state your mission and I need to tape you to do that. You can't expect me to preach." Bill stood and walked to the other side of the car so he could see Paul's eyes as they talked.

"Hey, you guys are lucky I didn't run over you. I could barely see the dome light on in the car. I've been calling your cell phone for an hour." Dennis Chapman spoke as he walked out of the fog.

"The battery is dead and the cord is broken. We have been waiting for you."

"Paul, are you all right?" Officer Chapman put his hand on Paul's shoulder.

"Yes, we're fine. How are you? How are the people at the mission?"

"Everyone is OK except three of the guys that came after you. One of them ran into your buddies with the baseball bats. I killed the other two when they pulled their guns and started blazing away. Very unprofessional. Did you figure out how they knew to come after you at the mission?" Chapman wiped his face with his hands and took a long deep breath.

"Bill thinks it was someone on his staff. They were the only ones that knew where he was and they knew he was coming to see me."

Paul gripped Dennis's arm and closed his eyes. "I am sorry someone had to die."

"Better them than you, or us, right, Bill?" Bill nodded his head. He was still deep in thought regarding Paul's words.

"Besides, it's part of my job. If they walk on my turf they better leave their guns in their yard. Let's get out of here. You never know. Someone could get lucky and find us here."

Bill looked to Paul and then to Dennis Chapman. "Where are we going?"

"To my house. You will be safe for the night and you can call your family from there in the morning. I can keep my eye on both of you easier there than any place else." Dennis started to walk toward his car somewhere in the fog.

"Why would you have to watch out for me, those guys came after Paul, don't you think?" Bill sounded worried.

Officer Chapman appeared out of the fog. "Yeah, but they used your name to get in." He vanished again into the fog but his voice continued. "Besides, with the responsibility Paul Iscariot just laid in your lap, I'm going to have to keep a close eye on you from now on."

Chapter 21
The Best in Man/The Worst in Man

THE FOLLOWING MORNING BILL was awakened by his cell phone ringing on the nightstand next to the bed. Dennis Chapman had an extra battery for the exact same phone Bill Larkin carried.

Bill answered, "This is Bill. Jane, where are you? What time is it?" Bill looked for his watch but it was not next to the phone. He looked around and saw Paul was gone. The bed he had slept in made and Paul's suitcase and duffel bag were not on the floor next to the bed. *This guy is some escape artist*, Bill thought.

"Bill, Bill, are you still there?" Jane was yelling into the phone.

"Yes, I'm here." Bill sat up and put his feet on the floor as he rubbed the sleep from his eyes.

"It's 6:45 in the morning. I'm at the office. I have been trying to get you all night. There were people killed at the mission last night and I knew you had gone there to meet the Healer. I have been extremely worried."

"Jane, how did you know I went to the mission?" Bill was wide-awake by now.

"Mark told me. After you left Jerry's, he called me and said you had a phone call from the Miracle Man and you went to the

LA Mission to meet him. Why?"

"How did Mark know I was at the mission?" Bill was standing, looking at the floor.

"I don't know, didn't you tell him?" Jane sounded worried.

"No, I didn't tell anyone. That was the deal I made to get the interview. Who did you tell, Jane? Someone told somebody else where I was and they came to the mission last night using my name at the door. Who did you tell?" Bill was pacing the floor and more angry than Jane had ever heard him.

"Just an old friend. Larry—"

Bill cut her off. "When the men arrived using my name, that's when the shooting started. Who else did you tell, Jane? Is getting ahead that God damn important to you, Jane Turner?"

"Jane, answer me, Jane. Jane." But it was too late. The phone call was discontinued from the other end. Bill threw the phone on the bed. It bounced twice and hit the headboard. He kicked his pants across the room and hit his fist into the door.

"Paul was right, you can't trust anyone." Bill walked into the kitchen. There was a note on the table.

> *Bill, I had to meet with some people this morning. I will be finished by 10:00 or 10:30. I would still like to give you the interview before I leave town. I am definitely leaving tonight. If possible, I would like to see Adrian once before I leave.*
> *Your Friend Paul Iscariot.*

Bill dialed his father-in-law's house and let it ring until Jack answered.

"Jack, Bill." Jack started right in with questions and concern about not hearing from him.

"I know. I know, it's a long story. I'm sorry I didn't have much of a choice. Was Susan worried?"

"No, she wasn't. But I sure was, Billy boy. I knew you were going downtown last night and it's bad down there. Even in the daytime." Jack was offering his help as well as concern.

"Thanks for the concern, Dad. Where is Susan now?"

"She went home with the boys and Elaine about fifteen minutes ago. She was going to get them dressed for school and pick up some things for Adrian and be back here around noon. I think she and Elaine were going to go to the beauty parlor before they came home. Is there anything I can do for you?"

"No, Jack, but thank you for offering. How is Adrian?" Bill sat back down on the bed.

"She's doing great. In fact, we were just about to dig into a huge stack of my pancakes, with melted butter and hot maple syrup. Why don't you come to the house and have some?"

"I would love to, but I can't right now, Jack. I need to finish my interview with Paul Iscariot. He said he would like to see Adrian before he leaves tonight, but I don't know. It's getting dangerous. The killings at the mission last night were because of Paul Iscariot."

"What killings at the mission?" Jack got serious.

"Have you seen the news this morning?" Bill knew Jack always had the news on when he fixed breakfast.

"Yes, I have the news on and there has been no word about a killing at the mission. Are you sure you're OK?" Bill couldn't figure it out.

"Yes, Jack, I'm fine. Listen, I don't know what to do about having Adrian see Paul tonight. I'll be in touch with you later. If anything comes up call my cell phone. I'll see you soon." Bill hung up before Jack could ask another question.

He started replaying the last several hours in his mind. *Chapman said there were multiple killings at the mission last night. Jane said she had heard of the killings. Jack said there was nothing on the news. A real press screwup unless, like this story, someone is keeping it from the press. But who and why?* The cell phone rang.

"Hello, this is Bill."

"Bill, Paul. I'm sorry I had to leave you so early. It looks like our meeting is going to be postponed indefinitely. I don't know how I can get to you in time. Word on the street is that someone wants me real bad. Bad enough to kill or be killed. Whoever it is sent those men to the mission last night.

"Chapman and two other officers are going to see that I leave town safely. I'm sorry it didn't work out. When the dust over this settles, I'll contact you and we can have a meeting in a jungle or rain forest somewhere. Anyplace where the only killers are tigers, snakes, or gorillas," Paul laughed.

"By the way, thanks for your help, Bill. Get involved in the rescue effort, Bill Larkin, you have more to offer than you know." Paul hung up the phone and Bill stared at his receiver. There was nothing he could do about it.

Bill showered and shaved. Dennis Chapman was definitely a bachelor, he thought. No woman could live in the conditions created by a man living the way he did. Once he was cleaned shaven and wide-awake, Bill headed for the office to tell Stan Eversol the circumstances and why he would be unable to share the greatest story of our day, with the rest of the world. His hunger overtook him and by 9:15 he was at a Coco's restaurant sampling their breakfast special. As the third and fourth bite were making their way down his throat, the cell phone rang.

"Hello, this is Bill." He took a gulp of coffee and chased it with water.

"Mr. Larkin, do you know of a man they call the Healer?" The voice was silent.

"Who is this?"

"That is not important. Let me inform you what is. I have your daughter and Jack sitting in front of me. They would like to have a word. Jack?"

"Billy, I'm sorry, kid. When the limo pulled up in front of the house and they said you sent them from the studio, you know, for the interview? Adrian and I got in and went with them."

"It's OK, Jack, is Adrian all right?"

"Daddy, is that you? This man said you are to bring the Healer, Paul, here to see him. Will you do that, Daddy? Will you please?"

"Adrian, honey, don't worry. Daddy will take care of everything." Bill clutched the phone with both hands. People in the restaurant were staring at him.

"That's touching, Mr. Larkin, but the only thing you must do is bring the Healer to me. When you are ready, call 213 555-7424."

"If you harm one hair on her head, a healer will not be able to save you, you son of a bitch. Do you hear me, you chicken-shit son of a bitch?" The phone was already dead. Everyone in the restaurant was staring at Bill and cowering in their seats.

He put $20 on the table and headed toward Chapman's house. He knew there must be a way for him to contact the officer and have him get word to Paul. It was his only hope. When he arrived there was a car in front of the empty house he had left only an hour ago. He rushed in and surprised a young woman half undressed. She screamed.

"I'm sorry. I didn't mean to scare you. Have you seen Dennis? It is urgent I speak with him immediately." The young woman held a sweatshirt in front of her to cover her naked breasts.

"No, I haven't seen him and who the hell are you busting in here like that."

"I know your father and I need to talk to him, it's a matter of life or death."

"If you know him, you should be able to contact him yourself. He has a pager."

Bill reached into his pocket and pulled out a pen and pad. "Can you give me the number please?"

The young woman started to relax. "What's your name?" She smiled and pulled the sweatshirt over her bare chest and stomach.

"Bill Larkin. What's yours?"

"Candy, Candy Sweet."

"Are you Chapman's daughter?" Bill was trying to warm her up to give him the phone number.

"Dennis's daughter, not a chance. He's a cop, you know." She put a piece of bubble gum in her mouth and started to chew loudly.

"Yes, I know he's a cop and I need to talk with him now." Bill stepped toward the phone.

"I'm a stripper. Dennis saved me from the drunk tank one night and took me home with him. He takes care of me when I need it and I take care of him every day. He's usually home now, I come by to serve him breakfast."

"He was here. I spent the night here last night with another man named Paul."

"Oh, you mean the Jesus guy? He's the nicest man I have ever met. But he's too pure to date a girl like me. Why do you want them?" Bill decided to be direct.

"My daughter has been kidnaped and I need Dennis and Paul's help to get her back safely. Will you help me?"

"On the level? Some SOB kidnaped your little girl? How old is she?"

"She's eight. Will you please help me, I need the pager number," Bill pleaded.

"Sure, Mr. Larkin, I'll give you the number." Candy went to a drawer and took out a clip of scrap paper put together like a directory. Dennis's pager number was under "P" for Police, according to Candy. Bill called it and entered his cell phone number. Five minutes later his cell phone rang.

"Chapman, it's Bill Larkin. I need to speak with Paul. Is he still with you?"

"Very good, Mr. Larkin. I was starting to worry about you. Who is Chapman?"

"How's my daughter? I swear to God I'll kill you if she's hurt in any way."

"No more threats, Mr. Larkin. There is nothing you can do to me except bring me the Healer! Now where is he?"

"I'm waiting for a call on this number. I don't know where he is."

"You were with him last night, weren't you?"

"Yes."

"Then call him now and bring him to me." The voice was impatient.

"He contacts me. I don't know where he is." Bill was thinking fast. What if Paul left town already and there was no way to reach him.

"I'm waiting, Mr. Larkin, and I am not a patient man. You have one hour or Jack and your little girl will be nothing more than a memory in your family album." With that he hung up.

The cell phone rang immediately. "Dennis, this is Bill. Is Paul with you?"

"Bill, where is Adrian? Elaine and I came home to see if Adrian wanted to go to the beauty parlor with us and she and Dad are gone. His car is here and the kitchen looks like they left in a hurry. Is she with you?" Susan spoke with a wave of panic accenting her question.

"No, Susan, she is not with me. We always said no secrets, correct?"

"Bill, where is Adrian?"

"Suz, she and Jack have been kidnaped and the kidnapper wants me to take Paul Iscariot to him. I don't know where Paul is but I am waiting for a call on this line from someone who knows where Paul is. Let me hang up. I'll call you the minute I know anything. Trust me, Susan. Trust me." He was pleading.

"Call me." Susan hung up as she started to cry.

The cell phone rang again. "This is Bill Larkin, Dennis?" It had to be him.

"Yeah, it's me. How did you get my pager number?"

"Candy. I'm at your house. Listen, someone connected with the trouble last night at the mission has kidnaped my daughter and her grandfather. The voice demanded to bring Paul to him or I would never see Adrian again." Bill started to break down.

"Bill, hold it together. Now is not the time to be weak. What else did the voice say?"

"He said time was critical. If I didn't call him back within the hour it may be too late." Bill composed himself and started to think.

"He gave you his phone number?" Chapman was surprised.

"Yes, he said it was the only way to save my daughter, I have to bring Paul to him as soon as possible."

"Paul is gone. I left him at his pickup point two hours ago. Do you think this voice knows what Paul looks like?"

"I don't know, why?" Bill already knew the answer.

"In order to get your daughter back, we'll have to be creative. Stay there. I can be there in fifteen minutes." With that Dennis broke off the connection.

Bill dialed the phone. It rang several times. "Come on, answer the damn phone."

A familiar voice answered, "Long Beach Rescue Mission, this is Gary Jenson, how can I help you?"

"Gary, Bill Larkin. I have been told Paul Iscariot has left town. You are my last hope. Some son of a bitch has kidnaped my daughter and her grandfather. He will kill them if I don't bring Paul to him within the next hour. Can you help me?"

"Bill, this is terrible news. I don't know what to say. I do know that Paul has gone. By now I don't think anyone can reach him. What will you do?"

"It looks like Dennis Chapman and I are going to tell the kidnapper one of us is Paul. We are going to gamble that the kidnapper doesn't know what Paul looks like. That will only buy us some time. I don't know what to expect. But if I get my hands on the bastard, I'll kill him."

"Are you with Chapman now?"

"No he is meeting me at his house in the next few minutes. When he gets here we'll call the kidnapper and follow his directions on what to do next."

"I have known Officer Chapman a long time. He will give his best, even if it includes his life, to save your daughter. Follow his orders exactly and you may come out of this thing with that which is most dear to your life. I will do what I can to reach Paul, but don't count on it." Gary Jenson was showing great concern.

"Where is your wife?" Gary asked.

"She's at my father-in-law's house. Why?"

"Give me the address, I will go to her and explain my confidence in Dennis Chapman. I will also pray with her." Gary was sincere.

"Thank you, Gary. I think that's a good idea." Bill gave him the address.

"What is the phone number there? In case any of my contacts reach Paul, I will have him call me. If you can, keep me updated on your progress with the kidnapper. I'll wait to hear from you."

Bill gave him the phone number. "Thank you, Gary. I will call as soon as I can."

As he hung up the phone, Chapman burst through the door. "Was that the kidnapper on the phone?" Chapman stripped off his shirt and his bulletproof vest.

"No, it was Gary Jenson. I called him to see if he knew how to get in touch with Paul. He is going to stay with my wife and mother-in-law."

"Jensen is a good man. If anyone can reach Paul it will be him. I have the plan all worked out." Chapman started to put on a pair of jeans, a white T-shirt, and a pair of work boots.

"Don't you think we should work out the plan together?" Bill stood over Chapman. Dennis stopped and stood face to face with Bill.

"After all it's my daughter." Bill backed away.

"First of all, this is how I make my living. Second of all, the men last night at the mission were professional. And third, we don't have a fucking clue what we're in for. Hell, I don't even know if we will wind up in my God damn jurisdiction. Do you?" Dennis sat down again and started dressing to look like Paul.

"No. Gary told me to trust you. But this is my daughter's life we're talking about and I don't want to risk losing her or her grandfather." Bill paced the floor.

"We don't have time to argue, so you're just going to have to go along with my plan. If you have any suggestions on improving it I will listen. But the final word is mine. Agreed?"

"Agreed." Bill stopped and faced Dennis Chapman.

"Take off your coat and shirt. Put that vest on and cover it so no one will notice you have it on." Chapman went to his closet. "Here, put this black tee shirt on over the vest first. The dark color will hide any lumps or seams. Here put this tie on too." Chapman threw him a wide tie. It looked like it came from the seventies; however, Bill did as he was told.

"You and I will go to wherever the kidnapper sends us. I will tell him I am Paul Iscariot. Except the kidnapper doesn't know Paul's name or what he looks like. The only one who knows Paul is Adrian. How old did you say she is?"

"She is eight and won't know not to give you away." Bill tucked in the shirt and put on his coat.

"I'll wear a ball cap and sunglasses. We will have to work on the element of surprise. It's our only hope. If she sees you first, well maybe she won't say anything about me." Chapman put on the glasses and the ball cap and looked surprisingly like Paul Iscariot, only bigger.

"What about last night? We know that if it's the same people, they won't hesitate to shoot you or me or even Adrian for that matter."

"I'll have a gun and you'll have my bulletproof vest. The important thing is to not let them know I'm a cop. Listen, newsman, we have no other choice.

"Do you want a gun? I assume you know how to use one

because of your service record. Am I wrong?" Dennis took a compact 9mm automatic from his dresser.

"I know how to use a gun." Bill checked to see if it was loaded and put in his waistband in the small of his back. He re-buttoned his shirt over the vest and gun. His coat fit loosely and hid everything very naturally.

"Let's hope you won't have to use it. Call the number."

Chapter 22
Beg To Die, Pray To Live

"THE VOICE SAID TO go to the Rich Plaza and someone will let us into the penthouse."

"I can't imagine anyone being able to get into the penthouse and hold hostages in the middle of a Friday morning." Dennis Chapman checked his pistol one more time and the two backup clips he had strapped to his leg.

"If I go down and you need more ammo, it's here on my leg. The clips are interchangeable. I have no idea what we are going to run into up there. But whatever happens, you shield your daughter. The vest will protect you from anything but a head shot. I'll do what I can to save us all. This is going to be strictly by the seat of our pants, old buddy."

"Do you think Thomas Rich has anything to do with this?" Bill was trying to figure out why they were to meet at the Rich Plaza penthouse.

"Who is Thomas Rich?" Chapman hadn't a due.

"He is the richest man in America, maybe the world. It's his building we're going to. You never heard of him?" Bill looked at the LA cop with disbelief.

"I work the harbor and the only thing I've ever seen is signs with the name Rich Fuels on them warning about underground pipelines."

"That is one of his companies." Bill pulled into the parking lot.

"This downtown stuff is too rich for my blood. I deal with scum crime. I rarely arrest anyone that has a car payment let alone a building with their name on it." Chapman was serious.

"This is the building. The voice said come without the police, come only with the Healer and take the elevator to the top floor marked 'P.' Someone will meet us at the elevator." Bill parked his car in one of the handicap spots in front of the building.

"That means someone will pat us down. If that happens, and they take my gun, I have a backup hidden where nobody living in this building will find it. If they get your gun too, we're up shit creek before we even get an oar in the water.

"As soon as the elevator doors open, I'll distract whoever is in the penthouse. If you can get to your daughter, do, and stay in front of her. I'll stall as long as I can until a course of action presents itself."

"Are you sure this is the best way to go about it? I'm trusting you with all of our lives, Dennis. Don't let me down." Bill stopped him and shook his hand.

"I'm sorry. I really do trust your decision." Bill turned and pushed the up button.

"Trust in God. Anything can happen up there today." Both men took a long deep breath. They rode the elevator in silence.

No one approached them until the elevator doors opened one floor before the penthouse. As the doors opened, a man stepped on. He was dressed like one of the men Chapman had killed the night before at the mission. Dennis and Bill stood in opposite corners with their backs to the wall.

The man pressed the button marked "P." As the doors closed the man turned and stood with his back to Bill and Chapman. He had an eerie grin on his face. When the elevator stopped, nothing happened. The door did not open.

The stranger in the elevator spoke first. "Are you carrying any weapons?"

"Fuck you!" Dennis responded. The man backhanded him in the mouth and reached around him, searching for a weapon until he found Dennis's gun.

"You must be the father of the little girl. What a brave man," the stranger said.

Bill spoke next. "I'm the father. Where is my daughter?"

"So the man of God carries a gun and says 'Fuck you'? We'll see about that."

Bill was afraid it was already out of control. Chapman's actions had taken the gate keeper off-guard and he didn't check Bill for a gun. The stranger, dressed in a dark business suit, put a plastic card into a slot in the elevator wall and the door opened. The three men entered a large penthouse, finer than anything Dennis Chapman had ever seen.

"Wait here." The man in the suit stepped through a side door and closed it behind him.

A tall man, with a perfectly tailored gray suit, walked into the room from a concealed door in the back of the large room. He had Chapman's gun in his left hand. Bill Larkin recognized him as Thomas Rich.

"Where is my daughter, you bastard?" He started to move toward Rich.

"No need for such hostility, Mr. Larkin. I'll see no harm comes to your daughter. I only needed her as an incentive for you and this so-called Healer to attend our impromptu meeting. You see, I'm dying and I have less than a day to find a cure."

With that Thomas raised the gun and shot Bill Larkin in the chest. Bill flew back against the elevator doors, hitting his head and collapsing in an unconscious heap.

"All right, Healer man, heal him."

Chapman bent over Larkin's body and could tell the vest had saved his life. He cracked an ammonia capsule under Bill's nose and Bill came to. Chapman helped him to his feet.

Bill held his chest, coughed and barely got out the words, "Where is my daughter?"

From the other side of the suite, Larry Dawkins brought Adrian into the room.

Bill walked slowly to her. Larry stood with his hands holding Adrian's arms tight against her back and kept her between himself and Bill Larkin.

Chapman had taken the pistol he had given to Bill from the waist of his pants while he was helping him up from the floor. Thomas Rich looked at the man he thought to be Paul Iscariot.

"Healer man, here's my proposition. I'm dying. Heal me and you all walk out of here alive and well with a million dollars in cash, each. Mr. Dawkins, let go of the girl and show them the cash."

Larry did as he was told. Adrian ran to her father and put her arms around his right leg. Thomas looked at Bill and Adrian.

"Mr. Larkin, your daughter's safe, sound, and without a scratch."

Bill knelt down and held Adrian tightly against his chest. Adrian, crying, put both arms around her father's neck and held on for all she was worth.

"Where's her grandfather?" Bill moved to a large sofa and put Adrian behind him knowing anything could still happen.

"He is my insurance policy, Mr. Larkin. If you accept my deal, he will join you at your in-laws' home within two hours after your departure. Do we have a deal?"

As Larry Dawkins opened one of the briefcases containing a million dollars, Dennis Chapman drew the gun from behind his back and shot Thomas Rich in the side of his face. Thomas went down hard behind his desk. Next he aimed his weapon at Larry Dawkins, who was unarmed.

"Get the little girl's grandfather or I'll kill you and find him myself."

Larry fell to his knees and pleaded for his life. "None of this was my doing. It was all Mr. Rich's idea. I had nothing to do with it other than following orders."

Thomas half crawled, half stood up behind the large desk

against the windows holding the gun in his left hand.

"Stop whining, you coward."

"Put the gun down, Mr. Rich," Chapman barked.

Just then a man came in from the side door firing an automatic sub machine gun. Chapman fell to the floor and dropped him before he hit anyone. Behind him the elevator doors opened. Chapman rolled to get a clean shot at whoever came through the doors and held his trigger finger when he saw it was Paul Iscariot.

"Paul, get down," Dennis yelled.

Paul walked into the room without hesitation. He stood in the middle of the room and looked at each person. "Bill, are you or Adrian hurt?"

"No, Paul." Bill took Adrian from behind his back and held her against his chest. "Chapman, you OK?"

"I think the guy with the automatic hit me in the leg. Other than that I'm fine. The guy behind the desk has a gun, don't go near him."

"The guy, you mean Thomas Rich?" Paul walked toward the heaving Thomas Rich.

"Who in the hell are you?" Thomas managed to get out between heavy breaths.

"I am the man you wanted to see so desperately that you would sacrifice an innocent child to see me. Why didn't you just ask for me at the mission?"

"I didn't know who you were. If you're the Healer, who is the man that just healed Larkin?"

Chapman struggled to get up on one knee, keeping his gun on Rich the entire time. "I'm a cop and Larkin has on a bulletproof vest."

Thomas began to cough and laugh at the same time. "You mean I was about to give my years of accumulated wealth to a fake?"

Paul walked closer to Thomas. "What do you mean, your wealth?"

"Larry, show him the documents." Thomas coughed up blood and fell back into his chair.

Larry Dawkins removed some papers from one of the briefcases. He handed them to Paul. "Once Mr. Rich signs these documents, you become sole beneficiary to his company's fortune. Upon his death that is."

"Yes, upon my death and not the death I am suffering at this moment. Upon my natural death."

Larry turned the pages. "Funds, totaling in excess of seven billion dollars, will be deposited in a trust of your designation and can be used in any manner you see fit."

Thomas coughed again as he told Larry to step back.

"But, only if you heal me now, Healer!" Thomas forced the arms of his dying body up onto the desk.

"This is a legal document?" Paul asked Larry.

"Yes, it is notarized and signed by Mr. Rich's legal counsel and there are three copies. There is also a copy of Mr. Rich's will stating the same and referring to this document. It is all in order."

"Sign it, Mr. Rich." Paul put it on the table in front of Thomas.

Thomas smiled. "How do I know you are not another fake like your friends over there?"

"You don't." Thomas dropped his left hand onto the desk. He still had the 9mm automatic in it. He fired into Paul's stomach. Paul fell to the floor dropping the duffel bag he had carried into the room from the elevator.

"God damn, you bastard." Bill rushed to Paul.

Thomas coughed again and smiled a bloody smile. "If he's a healer let him heal himself!" Thomas fell back into his chair again.

Paul pulled Bill's ear down close to his mouth. Bill listened as tears appeared on his cheeks. Paul continued to talk with a whisper into Bill's ear. When he was finished Bill Larkin lifted Paul to his feet. Paul looked at Thomas and spoke to him.

"Mr. Rich, I cannot heal myself, it will not work that way. But I can heal you. You sign the documents lying on the table and I will restore you."

Thomas stood with every bit of strength he could muster. "You heal me and I will sign my empire over to you, in front of these witnesses and before God, if you truly are a healer."

Paul looked at Larry, Larry nodded.

"Bill, help me over to Mr. Rich." Bill did as he was asked. Paul reached out and placed his right hand on the side of Thomas Rich's face where he had been shot. He closed his eyes and uttered an almost silent prayer. So soft was his voice no one in the room could make out what he was saying, other than the word forgiveness.

With his hand still on the face of Thomas Rich, his face began to heal. The blood on his face dried and the skin returned to its natural condition. Thomas was transformed. His strength returning as his face healed. Larry reached out and took the gun from his hand.

"Dawkins, am I healed? Can you see?" Thomas reached up to feel his face.

"Yes, as God is my witness you are healed."

Thomas turned to see himself in a mirror above the bar against the wall. "It's true—I am healed." Thomas turned back to Paul and picked up the pen from the desk. He started to sign the documents and then let the pen drop.

"Mr. Dawkins, I don't think this decision is in the best interest of our corporation, do you?" He turned to Larry Dawkins and smiled. Larry pulled back the hammer on the pistol in his hand and leveled it at Thomas's head.

"Sign it. If you don't, I will kill you myself. I will make it my last act on this earth to see you dead!"

"You weak bastard, Dawkins. You're fired!" Thomas picked up the pen and signed the documents. When he was through he handed them to Bill Larkin.

"Mr. Larkin, would you witness this transaction."

Paul crumbled, almost falling to the floor when Bill reached for the documents. With all of his strength he righted himself and leaned against the desk.

"Sign them, Bill. Put your name down as executor and have Mr. Dawkins sign them after you."

Paul watched as they carried out his orders. Bill handed one copy to Thomas and the other to Larry Dawkins. Larry folded it and looked at Paul.

"I will see to it that this document is followed exactly as it is constructed. Please forgive me for the part I played in this horrible act." Larry stepped back.

"You are forgiven."

Thomas was looking at himself in the mirror. He noticed his hands were still black but the pain was gone.

"Healer, where do you get your power?" Thomas turned toward Paul.

Paul spoke quietly into Bill Larkin's ear again. Bill moved Paul into Thomas's chair and retrieved the duffel bag Paul had carried into the room. He helped Paul open it and take out a bundle wrapped in what looked like old burlap cloth. Paul unrolled the cloth until the bundle came open showing a set of ancient tools.

"These are the tools Jesus used when he was a carpenter. It is from this sure knowledge that I draw my faith and pure faith is the source of my power. All that have come before me and all that shall come after me, share in this sure knowledge.

"Bill, see that my son receives these tools. He will know what to do with them and what is expected of him as I did when my father passed them on to me."

Thomas Rich moved to take the tools from the desk. Paul stopped him with a bloody hand.

"Mr. Rich, your hands will not touch these sacred tools. Your evil will not be rewarded this day or ever again."

Thomas withdrew and cringed at a pain in his chest.

"Paul, please use your power and heal yourself. Surely with

your faith and this knowledge you can heal yourself, can't you?"

Bill held Paul in his arms. Silently. Adrian had come over to Paul and was holding his hand. Paul closed his eyes.

"I made a decision today that prevents me from healing myself. I have taken another man's life. With that decision I cannot look into a child's eyes and proclaim I walk with God. Even God did not destroy the devil."

Bill put his hand to Paul's face. "But you have taken no man's life here today. Heal yourself."

Paul looked at Thomas Boy Rich. "The great wealth you have passed on will be a marvelous tool in the hands of my new executor." He looked next to Bill. "Gary Jenson has my instructions in the form of a will. He will explain how your life and the lives of your family will change forever to the service of mankind."

Thomas broke in. "Hold on, Healer. The documents we signed here today don't give you title to my money until I am dead of natural causes. Such as a heart attack or some incurable disease." Thomas stood up proud and strong like the statue in front of the museum. "You just healed me. I will be alive for another 20 or 30 years."

Paul spoke softly, barely able to utter his last words. "Mr. Rich, I healed your wounds, not your disease. Rest in Peace." With that Paul Iscariot died.

THE END